Mary Janeway

THE LEGACY OF A HOME CHILD

Mary Janeway

THE LEGACY OF A HOME CHILD

MARY PETTIT

NATURAL HERITAGE BOOKS
A MEMBER OF THE DUNDURN GROUP
TORONTO

Published by Natural Heritage Books
A Member of The Dundurn Group

Library and Archives Canada Cataloguing in Publication

Pettit, Mary, 1948-
   Mary Janeway : the legacy of a home child / written by Mary Pettit.

Includes bibliographical references.
ISBN 978-1-55488-413-1

   1. Janeway, Mary, 1887-1964--Fiction. 2. Home children (Canadian immigrants)--Ontario--Fiction.
I. Title.

PS8581.E8554M37 2009   C813'.6   C2009-900096-2

Edited by Laura Higgins and Jane Gibson
Design by Blanche Hamill, Norton Hamill Design
Printed and bound in Canada by Hignell Printing Limited, Winnipeg, Manitoba

Care has been taken to trace the ownership of copyright material used in this book. The author and the publisher welcome any information enabling them to rectify any references or credits in subsequent editions.
J. Kirk Howard, President

 Conseil des Arts   Canada Council   ONTARIO ARTS COUNCIL
du Canada   for the Arts   Canadä   CONSEIL DES ARTS DE L'ONTARIO

We acknowledge the support of the **Canada Council for the Arts** and the **Ontario Arts Council** for our publishing program. We also acknowledge the financial support of the **Government of Canada** through the **Book Publishing Industry Development Program** and **The Association for the Export of Canadian Books** and the **Government of Canada** through the **Ontario Book Publishers Tax Credit Program** and the **Ontario Media Development Corporation**.

Dundurn Press
3 Church Street, Suite 500
Toronto, Ontario, Canada
M5E 1M2

Gazelle Book Services Limited
White Cross Mills
High Town, Lancaster, England
LA1 4XS

Dundurn Press
2250 Military Road
Tonawanda, NY
U.S.A. 14150

To my parents, Robert and Gladys Hewson, for opening their hearts and their home to Mary Janeway, who in turn enriched all our lives.

"If, as psychiatry has told us, the years of our childhood are the years that shape our inner lives forever, then the practice of child emigration—the act of uprooting children and sending them, alone, across the ocean to work in a strange land in a strange occupation—must be regarded as one of the most Draconian measures in the entire history of children in English-speaking society. Its impact on the life of a sensitive child—even one who was placed in reasonable circumstances—is difficult to measure, sometimes difficult even to imagine."[1]

Kenneth Bagnell,
The Little Immigrants: The Orphans Who Came to Canada

"I don't know why they needed a girl…after all they had Annie. My grandparents never talked about Mary. My grandma was a bit hoity toity. I got the feeling that things weren't too good for Mary…you know she ran away."[2]

Joseph Jacques,
grandson of Daniel Jacques

ACKNOWLEDGEMENTS

Mary Janeway required extensive research in order to authenticate the historical context of the late 1800s in rural Ontario. I am indebted to many for their encouragement.

To Barry Penhale, my publisher, who took a long time deciding whether to publish my work but decided that Mary Janeway certainly 'deserved attention';

To Joseph Jacques, grandson of Daniel Jacques, for his willingness to share his past;

To David Lorente, Chair of the Heritage Renfrew Home Children Committee, for trying to help me locate Mary's name on juvenile immigration records and ship passenger lists. To David and Kay Lorente, for reading my manuscript twice for correctness;

To Kenneth Bagnell, author of *The Little Immigrants*, who willingly gave me permission to quote from his book;

To John Duncan, for his artistic ability in creating the sketches which help to tell my story;

To Barry Hoskins, publisher of Heritage Cards, for his photographs of the late 1880s and his artistic ability in scanning turn of the century photographs;

To Stella Clark, Branch Head of the Stoney Creek Library, and the staff of the Wentworth Libraries, for helping in my endeavour to research my subject thoroughly;

To Elizabeth Nelson-Raffaele, Curator of the Gibson House Museum, and Millie McClintock, Assistant Curator of the Historic Zion Schoolhouse, for kindly responding to queries about foodways and schooling in the 1890s;

To Joanne Reynolds, for fielding questions about nineteenth-century social customs;

To the Special Collections Department in the Hamilton Public Library, for their assistance while I sifted through the archives searching for authentic illustrations;

To Elizabeth Duern, English teacher at Saltfleet high school, for proofreading to identify the 'comma splices';

To George Milovanov, Head of the History Department at Saltfleet high school, for his advice on its historical authenticity and relevance to high school Canadian history;

To Gary Rawnsley, Eric Turner and Bill Stubbings, for their computer expertise and patience;

To Brian Carnahan, a freelance photographer for the Hamilton Spectator, who tried very hard to find my 'good side';

To Rosa, from Rosa's Day Spa and Silvana Elia, my hairstylist for their expertise and patience on 'photograph day';

To Laura Higgins of Natural Heritage for her quiet persistence in authenticating historical references and to Jane Gibson of Natural Heritage for her editorial experience;

To my best friend Catherine Steel, for her enthusiasm and willingness to proofread, chauffeur and be my research companion (and for the champagne when she witnessed the signing of my contract);

To my aunt, Beth Kelterborn, for always being able to answer the question, "Does this make sense?" and for her wisdom which only comes from years of life experience;

To my daughter, Allison, for her candid, honest but gentle criticism;

To my husband, Paul, for his faith in me that never wavered, even when mine did;

And finally to Mary Janeway, the little orphan girl who left her legacy behind because she trusted me with her story.

CONTENTS

Acknowledgements / ix

Author's Note / xiii

Prologue / 3

1. Home at Last / 7

2. First Impressions / 18

3. Settling In / 32

4. The Work Bee / 38

5. Mary's Birthday / 42

6. School Days / 45

7. Cat Gets a Name / 58

8. Christmas Pageant / 65

9. Mr. Murray's Visit / 72

10. A Family Reunion / 79

11. Back to School / 90

12. A Death in the Community / 103

13. The Community Celebrates / 111

14. Problems at the Gristmill / 119

15. Annie's Wedding / *129*

16. Mary Loses a Friend / *138*

17. Freedom at Last / *143*

Background to *Mary Janeway* / *150*

Endnotes / *156*

Glossary / *158*

Bibliography / *160*

About the Author / *162*

AUTHOR'S NOTE

Mary Janeway is a real person. Over time she told her stories to me. Innerkip is a town in rural Ontario, in Oxford County. The Jacques family did live outside of Innerkip.

Not all the characters, however, are real; I chose names for them at random while wandering through the Innerkip Cemetery one rainy afternoon. They are fictional and any resemblance to persons living or dead is purely coincidental. The book, *The Early Days of Innerkip District* by Zella Hotson, provided much of the historical context.

I have taken some literary liberties and indulged in some embellishments while conscious of preserving the integrity of my story. My intention was always to show compassion for the characters and record the events as accurately as my research and memory would permit.

Mary Janeway

THE LEGACY OF A HOME CHILD

PROLOGUE

October 1889

FROM A distance, the silhouette of the gnarled wooden clothesline post leaning into the wind looked like a tired, hungry traveller. Upon closer inspection, you could see it had been weathered smooth through countless storms.

She stooped to pick up the last pair of overalls to be hung on the line. The clouds were dark to the west, but she hoped the storm was a couple of hours away. October winds from the moors were strong and would likely dry the clothes before the rain came. A small, scrawny child in a long brown pinafore appeared out of nowhere and ran barefoot toward the woman.

"Pick me up, Mama. It's coming, it's coming!" she screamed. The woman, who looked to be about eight months pregnant, quickly hung the overalls on the line, bent down and scooped her daughter into her arms.

"Mary, you mustn't be afraid. The rain will make the flowers bloom," she laughed. The child was silent and comforted momentarily, at least. The mother worried about her five-year-old's fear of storms, but with four others to tend to, she didn't have much time to think about it.

She held the little girl close to her swollen belly. "Without rain, why the earth would dry up, nothing would grow and we would surely die," she spoke in a quiet, more serious voice. Having said that, she plunked the child into the wooden basket and carried her back to the house.

"Shh, don't fuss or we'll wake Emma," she whispered to Mary as they went inside. Emma, Mary's little sister, asleep in the crib, was almost two.

Carolyn was sitting by the window doing her favourite thing, needlepoint. She was eleven, very artistic and the eldest child in the Janeway family. Whenever Mama was sick or having a baby, Carolyn was in charge. It was not something she liked, but it was expected of her. She looked forward to leaving home when she turned sixteen.

Will and John were chattering away and playing checkers on the floor beside the sofa in the front room. Considering they were just over a year apart, they got along well. Will, the elder of the two, was quite grown up for a nine-year-old boy.

As a very young child in 1886, Mary Janeway may have resembled this young English girl. *Barry Hoskins, Heritage Cards.*

Mary adored her mother and went right into the kitchen to help. Climbing onto a little round milk stool by the sink, she began to scrub potatoes and carrots for supper. Mary knew how to set the table, dry dishes and make her bed. She also arranged the toys in Emma's crib every morning without being asked.

The Janeways lived in Rutherglen, Scotland, almost three miles outside of Glasgow, a city with a population of 1382. Their home was in a pretty little rural area, but the winters were harsh and long. Sometimes one did not venture out for days for fear of freezing to death. Everyone worked so hard to prepare for the one season they dreaded that the others passed too quickly.

As the Janeway children rarely saw other people, they relied heavily on each other for companionship. Mary enjoyed each one of her brothers and sisters, but her heart had been stolen by John. No-one was really sure why, but everyone knew it was so.

William and Catharine Janeway were a hardworking, God-fearing couple whose only ambition in life was to eke out an existence for their ever-increasing family. William worked as an apprentice surveyor, often gone for weeks dealing with surveys for new roads and bridges. When he was home, he worked his small acreage, tended to his sheep, chickens and his two draught mares. While he was away, Catharine ran the household, and with help from the boys, cared for the farm. Although they were poor, they loved their children and they believed the hand of the Almighty would guide them through troubled times. So far their faith had paid off. Carolyn had been saved from the croup, Will from nearly drowning in the peat bogs and Mary from being burned during a lightning storm that destroyed their barn, a year ago almost to the day.

"Carolyn, please set the table. Papa will be in from his chores shortly and he'll be hungry," Mama said. Carolyn got up reluctantly but said nothing.

Mary worked steadily at the sink, but something moving caught her eye through the kitchen window. It was Papa running to the house, holding his hands over his face. His hands were soaked with blood!

Mary screamed. Her mother ran to the window and gasped. When he stumbled through the door, each child in turn became motionless and silent as though frozen in place. Catharine grabbed her apron from the hook and ran to her husband. "Oh my God, William!" she cried. His nose was hanging broken and he was bleeding badly. Before he could explain how the colt had reared up and kicked him, his pregnant young wife, overcome with emotion, fainted on the kitchen floor.

"Catharine!" he screamed as he bent over her. "Help me carry her to the bed," he shouted at the children. "Will, run to Packard's farm and tell Lyle to get the doctor quick. Mama needs help real bad."

Little Mary had been watching everything. She stepped down off the stool, backed into the corner, crouched down and buried her face in her knees. Emma began to cry.

The next morning Papa called all the children, including Emma, to the table. He had bandages on his face. "We lost Mama in the night. The baby came sudden—far too soon for your mama. She wasn't strong enough." He paused to steady himself, and then continued reluctantly. "The doctor was too late to do anything. The baby's gonna live but it's small and sickly. He thinks it isn't quite right so they're sending it to Glasgow. Just as well I expect." He continued, but spoke quietly. "I love you all and I'll try to take care of you, what with Mama gone now."

A week later, Papa gathered his children in the kitchen once more. He looked tired and drawn, the dark rings under his eyes making his face look even more pale. The older children could feel his tension, but little Emma continued to prattle in her crib. He scarcely knew how to begin.

"Carolyn, well, you're near old enough to fend for yourself." He hesitated, then took a big breath. "Doc thinks it's best if the rest of you go to the London Fields Hackney Home. They'll take good care of you." William put his head down and covered his face with his hands. "Don't be thinkin' this is easy, cause it ain't," he said.

One

HOME AT LAST

"Between 1870 and the depression of the 1930s,
more than 80,000 children from the British Isles
journeyed to Canada in an extraordinary but almost
forgotten odyssey. They were known as the "home
children," but beneath that benign description was a
story of lonely and forlorn youngsters to whom a
new life in Canada meant only hardship and abuse."[3]

November, 1889

THE LONDON Fields Hackney Home was a government-run Christian
Juvenile Home-for-the-Homeless that looked after children from infancy
to age fourteen. The home was always short of money and operated on a
minimal budget, subsidized by grants and charitable organizations. Need-
less to say, the overworked and underpaid staff were not likely to be overly
sympathetic and kind to their young charges. This was not a happy place for
anyone. Abruptly removed from their childhood home and still grieving for
their mother, the Janeway children suddenly found themselves among
strangers in a grimly austere and dingy building on a narrow crowded
street. They had never been in a city before.

Within four weeks of the Janeways' arrival at the orphanage in November 1889, Will ran away, telling absolutely no one of his plans. Mary was

Taken from an original broadsheet advertising Mrs. Birt's Sheltering Home. *Courtesy National Archives of Canada, C-4690 Vol. 32 File 724 Part 1.*

devastated. With no idea where he had gone, she tearfully wondered if she would ever see him again. Valiantly, the three remaining Janeways tried to protect one another, but there was more to come.

In early January and without any warning, Mary and John were separated from Emma and sent to the "Sheltering Home" on Myrtle Street in Liverpool. Their days were filled with routines that never varied, the regimentation unfortunately too common in institutional settings. A Protestant-run home for orphans, fatherless, motherless and destitute children,

POVERTY TO PLENTY.

How charming the change that awaits poor fatherless, motherless, or friendless boys and girls, who are fortunate enough to be taken to Canada, out of the wretchedness and poverty that surrounds them in Liverpool to a country life, with abundance of all they need, giving them health and strength, and making into useful, sober, and industrious men and women those who would otherwise die prematurely, or lead stunted, starving, blighted lives.

Co-operation from all who can help will be gratefully accepted by Mrs. Birt, at the new premises in Myrtle Street.

Office Hours:—10 to 4 o'clock any day.

NUMBERS.—More than three thousand poor, hungry children have been made clean, happy and respectable by the good training they have had under Mrs. Birt's care; about 2,500 of these have had a complete and substantial outfit of clothes, situations and homes in Canada provided for them, and are now doing well.

Wages.—They are in receipt of good wages in Canada, and are much better off there than they ever could have been in Liverpool, surrounded by poverty and misery. Many have done extra well, being bright, intelligent children. Quite a number of boys are now in various positions of trust and honour, such as ministers, missionaries, doctors, dentists, clerks, foremen, shopkeepers, tradespeople, farmers, and girls as mother's helps, learning to be capable in a house and home, are earning better wages than they could get here, and some of them have money in the bank.

Interesting editorial copy of the late 1880s extolling the virtues of the Sheltering Home and its program. Financial security was considered to be of the utmost importance. *Courtesy National Archives of Canada, C-4690 Vol. 32 File 24 Part 1.*

the Sheltering Home was entirely supported by voluntary contributions. Here again, there was barely enough to provide food and shelter, another bleak and dreary existence for the remaining siblings. Everything at the home was run according to very strict rules. Even the visiting hours were clearly defined and adhered to with absolute strictness. All the orphans were under Mrs. Birt's care. Her goal was simple—to find homes for them in Canada. Both Mary and John, but Mary especially, fretted over the forced separation from their baby sister. It was not until Emma turned four, almost two years later that the little family was reunited.

———————

Almost two and a half years after her arrival at the Sheltering Home, Mary filled her battered little red valise once again. All three of them, plus others at the Sheltering Home, had been lined up one day and herded through a physical check-up given by a doctor from the Liverpool Hospital for Consumption and Diseases of the Chest. Vaccinated, pronounced in good health and free from all disease and defects, the Janeway children were about to become little immigrants. It was a frail, hesitant seven-year-old child that boarded the *S.S. Carthaginian* bound for Canada along with her brother and younger sister that cold, dreary day in March of 1892.

Two hundred and twenty-nine souls were on board that steamship— one hundred and eighty-six adults, thirty-seven children and six infants. Only twenty-seven were cabin passengers; the rest were to be put in steerage, the dark, unventilated bowels of the ship. There they would spend their journey across the ocean, crowded together beneath the deck of the ship. All of the orphans, including Mary and her siblings, were steerage passengers, packed below along with the other poor less fortunate emigrants, a total of 202 people about to embark on a grim journey to the New World.

A sketch to represent the *S.S. Carthaginian*, based on the ocean liner *City of New York* by James G. Taylor (New York Historical Society). This ship was launched in the late 1880s. *Sketch by John Duncan.*

Home Children Passenger Lists

JANEWAY , William

Age:	8
Sex:	M
Year of arrival:	1891
Microfilm reel:	C-4538
Ship:	SS Sarnia
Port of departure:	Liverpool
Departure Date:	5 Jun 1891
Port of arrival:	Quebec
Arrival Date:	15 Jun 1891
Party:	Stratford (and Hamilton)
Destination:	Mary THOMPSON, domestic to Hamilton.

A search of passenger lists located William Janeway, Mary's older brother. The rest of the Janeway children were not indexed and could not be found. It is speculated that Mary and her siblings left England in 1892. *List courtesy National Archives of Canada C-4538.*

As was the standard of the day, living conditions in steerage only just met the government requirements, and no more. Each passenger was to have sufficient drinking water and food. The food was plain: potatoes, fresh bread and meat for as long as stores lasted, and tea. On Sundays there was a treat—pudding.

Women, appointed by the authorities in England, were there to provide some support for the women and children, and the captain was expected to visit daily. While there were to be provisions made for the disposing of human waste, the only toilets in steerage were open buckets, with no privacy. These were carried up and emptied overboard daily. Sanitary conditions were deplorable and without enough water for personal washing. To make matters worse, the children, along with many of the others, were seasick a great deal of the time. With each passing day, the stench below deck grew steadily more foul.

Rarely did the sun shine, but when it did, the children who were well enough were allowed to go up on the deck. Their innocence helped them set aside their sorry plight long enough to invent a form of tag which could be played in the open air on the wooden deck of the massive five-hundred-foot-long ship. More commonplace, however, was bad weather, frigid temperatures and fierce winds. Then the hatches would be battened down as the huge vessel heaved from side to side, the movement creating fearsome creaks and moans. These eerie sounds alone, especially in the darkness of steerage, were sufficient to terrify even the most brave, but the fear of fire prevented their lighting candles during most of the voyage. Often the children clung to each other for support and comfort in the darkness.

Soon they learned ways to help each other and pass the time. The older children helped feed the younger ones. With imagination and memories of childhood games, they fashioned splinters of wood and fragments of rope into hours of fascination. Tremendous pressure was put on the older ones to protect the "young...uns." Many nights Mary would fall asleep in the arms of her older brother, while she, herself, cuddled Emma.

After some twenty-three treacherous days at sea, the S.S. Carthaginian docked in the Montreal harbour one morning in mid-April. Photographers were standing by on the dock as the steamer was secured and its dirty and bedraggled steerage occupants were herded off like cattle. Both the ship and its travellers appeared anxious for a well-deserved rest. Those who had survived the journey, two hundred and twenty-seven to be exact, plus a newly-born infant, a little boy, born prematurely to a mother of four travelling in steerage, moved slowly down the gangplank.

The young children exuded anxiety and trepidation. Their wide-eyed stares and thin, haggard faces spoke eloquently of their strenuous ocean crossing, and made a compelling picture. Their tragic story could be told over and over again in hopes of finding homes for these orphans.

Four-year-old curly-headed Emma was in John's arms. Mary followed close behind, clutching his coat tail. They stood almost rooted to the spot when their feet touched dry land. A newspaper photographer snapped their picture in that instant before they were caught up in the crush of the crowd. It was to be their last family photo.

A small group of government officials awaited their arrival. An older gentleman with a dark handle-bar mustache took charge. With an officious sounding voice, he cleared his throat and read aloud; "Those under five years of age will go with Mrs. Raynor and be in her charge."

A small, plump lady standing at his side raised her hand as a way to identify herself and, along with several young women, she proceeded to pluck the youngsters from the crowd. John gave Emma a quick hug, kissed her on the forehead and handed her to one of the women. Emma, clutching the scruffy little rag doll that Mary had given her, began to cry. Mary stood motionless and watched in quiet desperation. She had no idea that they were to be separated once again. As tears began to roll down her cheeks, Mary's shoulders began to slump in despair. With that, John protectively took her by the hand.

"The following girls will be sent to Stratford under Mr. Murray's charge."

Mr. Murray, a tall serious-looking gentlemen in his forties, was an inspector from the agency office in England, sent to Canada to run the "Distributing Home" in Stratford. He stepped forward while the names were read aloud. Mary was in a daze but quickly realized her name must have been called because John clenched her hand even tighter and started to move toward the group of girls that was forming.

"No, John, please don't leave me. I want to be with you. I'll be good as long as I can stay with you. Please, John! Please!" Mary begged him as she gripped his hand tighter.

John's blue eyes, the same cobalt blue as Mary's, filled with tears as he pried her fingers loose and literally handed her over to Mr. Murray who grasped her hand firmly. John bent down, grabbed his sister by both shoulders and whispered, "I have to, Mary. I ain't got no choosing in the matter. Pa said." He bit his lower lip, got up and turned away. John never looked back at the sobbing child, for he was crying himself. This memory stayed with Mary for years, often recurring in nightmares that would awaken her from a fitful sleep. She would play out the scene in her mind time and time again, re-experiencing the empty feeling the parting left inside.

Along with a handful of girls approximately her age, Mary was taken to Stratford, Ontario. Here she would stay at the Strathcona Home for Girls, and for some time be under the care of Mr. Murray, until a suitable placement could be found. A temporary shelter for girls between the ages of five and eighteen, the home endeavored to place girls with families in need of a domestic.

Less than two months after her arrival, Mary was summoned to the parlour. She had never been in this room before. While somewhat frightened for fear the directive should mean she was in trouble, she was also excited. It could mean that, finally, she would have a home. Little did Mary realize that the following scene would affect her for the rest of her life.

She entered the room cautiously. The parlour had a dark, red carpet, and was furnished with several large wing chairs and a pretty floral settee. Her eyes widened as she tried to take in all she could. Never had she seen such a beautiful room. She saw lots of fancy trinkets and photographs, a fireplace and a smoker placed near a very comfortable looking maroon armchair. A vase of yellow flowers had been set in the middle of a little table. Standing near the fireplace was Mr. Murray, and beside him a stranger.

The stranger was almost six feet tall, with a reddish-brown scruffy beard and mustache. Wearing somewhat shabby grey pants and a coat, the man had his hands crossed in front of him. He was holding a black hat. Awed by the sight, Mary stopped and looked up.

Mr. Murray broke the silence. "Come in, Mary. Don't be shy. This is Mr. Jacques. He has a farm nearby and needs a girl. You will be going to live with him and his family." He paused for a moment, and then continued with a smile. "You're lucky to find a home so quickly. Now run upstairs and collect your belongings. Mr. Jacques would like to leave right away."

Mary said nothing and neither did Mr. Jacques. Silently turning away, she left the room and went upstairs. Mr. Murray held up the letter he had written which authorized Mr. Jacques to take Mary into his custody. A signature was required. The farmer looked at the letter for a moment and handed it back.

"I never had much schooling, just three days. Didn't care for it and never went back."

Mr. Murray did not react to this news in any way. His job was to place the children, not be judgemental. So he proceeded to read the letter to Mr. Jacques:

"I, Daniel Jacques do hereby and herewith, God being my helper, take in Mary Janeway, an orphan with no family. I promise to provide a good Christian home and to feed, clothe and shelter her to the best of my ability. I also promise that she will be sent to school, weather permitting, until the age of sixteen. In return I expect the child to work diligently, be respectful and obedient. An inspector from the federal government will visit once a year and talk to the child in private, at which time he must be satisfied the child has been obedient, been given enough food and clothing and an adequate place to sleep. In witness whereof I have hereunto set my hand, on the sixth day of June, in the year of our Lord one thousand eight hundred and ninety-two. Signed, Sealed and Delivered in the presence of us."[4]

Mr. Murray set the document on the table, handed Mr. Jacques a quill pen and put his index finger on a blank spot on the paper, Mr. Jacques marked it with an "X."

———————

Mary threw what little she owned into her old and battered red suitcase, now held together by a thick leather strap. Besides her best dress, the little pink and yellow flowered pinafore which she put on, she owned two dresses she had inherited at the orphanage. One was a faded grey colour and far too long on Mary. She had already been told numerous times, "You'll grow into it." Why would she want to? She hated it. The other one was brown and white and although she didn't like the colour much, at least it fit her. Her winter coat, long since outgrown, had been left behind before her voyage to Canada. She had three pair of underwear, three undershirts, a pair of socks, shoes that were almost too short and one and a half flannel nighties. The half nightie which was too small for Mary now, had only one arm in it and the flannel was worn paper-thin. But it was her favourite. It had been a Christmas present from her parents a few years ago, the last Christmas they had together. Other than a now much-worn photograph, the nightgown was the only reminder that once she had been part of a family.

Mary held the dog-eared picture in her hand. She sat and looked at it

a long time before carefully placing it underneath her clothes in the suitcase. A photograph, taken by a visiting friend, showed a tall, skinny dark-
haired boy holding a chubby toddler on his lap. Of course, Mary had been
too young at the time to remember any of the circumstances. Ma had told
her about it much later. She could remember as though it were yesterday.

*Mary climbed on Mama's lap when Emma finally fell asleep. It meant that
she could spend a few minutes with her alone. Mama affectionately wrapped
her arms around her daughter and squeezed her tightly.*

    *"Mary, when you were born, John was so happy." She let out a big sigh. "You
were real tiny. Most were afraid to touch you, never mind hold you. Not John.
He acted as if he knew you were special right from the beginning. And he was
right. Why, he helped to care for you. It was almost as if you were his baby.
Now you'll understand that picture better," she said, kissing the top of her
curly head tenderly. Mama loved telling that story over and over again as
much as Mary loved to hear it.*

Finally Mary packed a small rubber ball. Each child at the orphanage had
been given one last Christmas and cautioned not to lose it. It was her only
toy. She thought about the cloth rag doll she had treasured as a baby, and
had given to her little sister Emma the day they parted company in the
Montreal harbour. Despite her young age, she knew she must not dwell
on painful reminders.

    Mary shut her suitcase carefully. One latch worked and the strap helped
close the other side. She always insisted on carrying it, even if someone
offered to help her, for fear it would spill open. She picked the case up
with ease; it was light. Mary walked gingerly down the stairs, as prepared
as could be, speculating on what new venture might be in store for her.

    What kind of person was Mr. Jacques? He had scarcely said a word.
What was his family like? How long would it take to get there? Where
would she be sleeping tonight?

    By now some of the girls had quietly clustered around the hallway.
Mary said goodbye to her friends. No-one cried. They were used to fare-
wells by now. As she shook Mr. Murray's hand, he said, "I'll visit you next
spring to see that things are working out. Goodbye, Mary."

    "Goodbye, Mr. Murray," she replied politely and headed for the horse and buggy where Mr. Jacques was waiting. A man of few words, he did not say anything as he helped her into her seat. As they headed down the road, it was an interesting sight they made—horse and buggy and the silhouettes of two figures: one a tall, lean man wearing a hat and the other, a frail curly-headed little child.

As they drove out of Stratford, Mary sat bolt upright. Her mind began to race as her apprehension grew. What will this place look like? Will there be children? Will I share a room? How long will I stay? And most important, will they like me?

The two hour buggy ride to the Jacques farm on the outskirts of Innerkip seemed endless, with only one brief stop made to rest the horse. Mr. Jacques had been silent for the entire trip, speaking only to the horse as necessary. When they finally arrived, Mary was tired and anxious. It was nightfall and difficult to see what the place looked like. Except for a small lamp in the front window, the whole house was in darkness. No-one was there to greet her. One can imagine—a little fair-haired girl with the large frightened eyes, clutching her suitcase and climbing the narrow staircase in a strange house, following the tall silent man, not knowing what would happen next.

Mr. Jacques took Mary directly to her room, said it was time for bed and left abruptly. The room was a small alcove directly above the kitchen. There was a cot, a straw tick mattress, one thin grey blanket, a pillow and a tiny cupboard for her clothes. The sparseness was not a problem. Mary owned so little.

She undressed quickly and climbed into bed. She wasn't hungry even though all she had eaten that day was a bun and a piece of cheese that Mr. Jacques had given her during the trip. She was tired, her legs ached and she had a feeling of uneasiness. Just to be on the safe side, Mary got out of bed and knelt beside her cot. The only light coming into the room was from a slice of the faraway moon and it cast a foreboding yellow glow on the young child's profile.

Mary's voice was shaky. "Dear God,—I hope they will like me. I promise to be good. I want to go to school and have a real teacher." She got up and started to get in bed, then faltered and dropped down on her knees again. "Amen," she whispered. Mary had been taught not only to say her prayers but to say them properly, or they didn't really count.

Two

FIRST IMPRESSIONS

"Some were children barely out of arms and were
therefore adopted, but most—more than nine thousand—were past their fifth birthday and in this hard
land were expected to earn their keep, tending barns,
milking cows, making hay. Often they would rise
before anyone in the house, before the first light of
day, and they would work until nightfall."[5]

June 10, 1892, Friday

MARY WAS awakened suddenly in the early hours of the morning by
four pair of eyes staring at her from the doorway of the loft.

"That's her," whispered the smallest of the boys, pointing a finger in her
direction. Mary turned her head away and lay cowering against the wall.
She said nothing. When she looked again, they were gone. She got out of
bed, dressed quickly and went cautiously down the stairs. She was curious
but at the same time fearful of what lay ahead.

Mr. Jacques was at the kitchen sink. He turned and smiled, "Good
mornin'."

Then she heard a voice from the far corner of the room near the stove.
It was a woman who looked much younger than Mr. Jacques. Seated in a
bulky chair with a large wheel on either side, she was almost totally
wrapped in a blanket even though it was a fine June morning.

"I don't know what time you're in the habit of rising, but here, you are to be the first one up, not the last." The woman spoke with a crisp tongue. Mary was stunned and speechless. Not only did the sharpness of tone catch her off guard, but she was curious about the unusual chair. Timidity kept her from asking.

"I'm Mrs. Jacques. I'm in charge. You're to call me Ma'am." Turning slightly in her chair and motioning toward the wood stove, she continued. "In the winter you are to rake off the ashes and start the fire from the coals the minute you rise. Of course, it isn't necessary in the warmer months. Only time you'll need a morning fire then is when we bake bread, every Wednesday." Within a short period of time, Mary would come to dislike Wednesdays. Baking bread was no job for a young child. "You'll find the woodpile out back." Mrs. Jacques continued and pointed towards the door. "Make sure the woodbox is always full. There are two pumps outside, one for the cistern and one for the well. Fill the reservoir in the stove with water from the rain barrel and fill the kitchen pail with well water morning and night."

Without pausing, but looking Mary right in the eye, she went on, "I expect the kitchen floor swept every morning once the fire is lit. There are two brooms in the shed outside the door, a corn broom and a hickory one. I don't care which one you use. The dogs need to be fed every night by five. Set the table for six and a place at the end for you." Mrs. Jacques pointed to the far end of the pine table. "I laid out one place so as you could see how it's done. I expect it to look like that. Dishes are on the shelf." Mary's eyes followed the woman's hands as she issued the orders and pointed in various directions.

"Have you ever made oatmeal?" Mrs. Jacques asked.

"No."

"It's no, Ma'am."

"No, Ma'am," Mary replied.

"I'll show you tomorrow. I can't do everything today. Breakfast must be ready by seven. The boys leave for school at seven-thirty. Do you have any questions?"

"Can I go to school too, Ma'am?" she asked in a quiet, apprehensive voice.

"Not much point starting now. There's only a week or so left and I don't imagine much learning is going on. We'll see about it in the fall." She paused. "And besides, you'll be real busy right here."

CENSUS OF CANADA, 1891.														

Taken from the census records of 1891, showing the names of the Jacques sons. *Courtesy National Archives of Canada, T-6360.*

Mary's eyes dropped. Disappointed by this news and overwhelmed by her array of abrupt orders, she had difficulty hiding her dismay.

"Don't be sulking, Girl. Get yourself some oatmeal, sit on that stool by the corner and I'll explain your other chores," she said with a slight smile. And so the day began.

Mary was walked through a routine that would soon become all too familiar. Her days would seem endless and her whole being consumed by repetitive, tedious tasks. When one chore was complete, another was waiting to be done.

Mary was not formally introduced to the Jacques children until several days after her arrival. It was Sunday morning and the family was getting ready to go to church.

Annie Marie, the eldest and the only girl, was eighteen and a dutiful daughter. She had dark hair like her mother but was taller and smaller boned. Annie had a forceful, abrupt manner which matched her height. Having finished elementary school, Annie was working in James Malcolm's cheese factory nearby, returning home from work each night. It was considered improper for a girl to leave home for any reason other than to get married. By the time a girl was eighteen she was referred to as a spinster, but Annie's mother refused to acknowledge the fact that her only daughter was an "unclaimed treasure." She'd had two quilting bees for her and the quilts were stored in a cedar chest anticipating the arrival of an acceptable suitor. It was a subject that was not discussed.

Annie's one love was to work in the garden, and even though she

THE JACQUES FAMILY TREE [6]

Daniel Jacques   =   Mary Elizabeth Mundy
Feb. 5, 1836–   April 19, 1856–July 7, 1912
July 14, 1921

Annie Marie   =   Elias Zinkan
b. Feb. 11, 1875

Gordon   Beverley   Ruby   Doris
                       b. 1911

Thomas   =   Edith Town
b. May 26,
1877

Earl   Clara May

Christopher   =   Eva
b. April 24,
1880

Elmer

Daniel Jr.   =   Jane Chesney
April 29, 1882–   1891–1975
July 4, 1932

Joseph Leslie   =   Evelyn Moyer
b. June 3, 1911

Mary Maria   =   William Skillings
1920–1995

Patricia   Thomas   Bruce   Donna
Mary   William   Wayne   Marilyn

worked long hours at the cheese factory, she still found time to manage a large vegetable garden of corn, beans, squash and potatoes. She also liked to cook and had been a great help to her mother in the last few years. However, the day-to-day food preparation would now become Mary's responsibility and would leave Annie more time to tend her garden or make the family favourites like johnnycake and apple snow.

Annie's first comment to Mary was, "You're awfully small. I sure hope you're strong or what possible good will you be to my mother?" She turned toward her mother for approval as she spoke.

The three boys, even finer boned than their sister, included sixteen-year-old Thomas who said very little, thirteen-year-old Christopher who was even quieter, and Daniel who had just turned eleven. Daniel, named after his father, was the most outgoing. He was also the animal lover, which explained the two dogs. Tiny was a scrawny hound that Daniel had found last winter in a field, dying of starvation, and Ben, a brown and white spotted beagle, was one of the Skillings pups, given to him on his ninth birthday. Neither animal was allowed in the house, much to Daniel's disappointment. His mother had allergies to animal fur. So the dogs stayed in the barn at night, if in fact they decided to come home at all. By day they wandered at will.

Mary felt perhaps Daniel might become her friend. She was sorry that there were not more girls in the family since a friendship with Annie seemed obviously out of the question.

Very quickly, Mary learned the routines of the Jacques family. On Saturday night, baths were taken by each member of the family. It was believed that bathing too frequently would remove those body oils which helped to prevent people from getting sick. Besides, heating the water required much time and effort. Since there was no bathroom in the house, they took turns taking a bath in the dubious privacy of the kitchen which was the warmest room in the house. A large wooden tub was set in the middle of the kitchen floor, half filled with warm water. Mr. Jacques was first and a little warm water was added for each newcomer, beginning with the oldest child, Annie, then descending in chronological order to the youngest. Mary was always last. On bath evenings, Annie helped her mother with a basin of water in her bedroom.

Monday was "wash day," but clothes were worn many times before they were considered dirty. The Jacques were cautious not to wash things unnecessarily since they would wear out faster and need to be replaced.

The outhouse, or privy as the Jacques called it, was a little log shanty, "just a piece" removed from the house and used year round. Since outdoor work fell to the men, it was the job of one of the Jacques boys to throw a cupful of Gillett's lye down the hole and see that there was an outdated Eaton's catalogue and a supply of old newspapers there at all times. With the exception of Mrs. Jacques, the entire household used this privy.

Mary witnessed lots of outhouse pranks. Thomas and Chris would lock their younger brother in on a regular basis, but he outsmarted them as he got older. Mary would never forget the time he scaled the walls, got out by scrambling through a hole in the roof and hid in his room until supper. When his brothers went back to unlock the door, much to their amazement, he was not to be seen. They were convinced he had fallen in. Daniel appeared at the dinner table but not until after they had confessed to "losing" him down the hole in the privy. Both boys had to do Daniel's chores for a week.

Gillett's lye was used to keep the privy or outhouse sanitary during the summer months. For over 100 years, their advertising slogan has been : '12 ways to "Lye" effectively' will show you what a big difference a "little white Lye now and again can make in your life." *Courtesy Joseph Aziz, President, Gillett's Cleaning Products Inc.*

The boys also loved to tease Annie when she was in there after dark by making weird animal noises in the woods or suddenly banging on the door. Just as suddenly, they would run away and, of course, if suspected, would deny any such suggestion.

During the night, chamber pots, one under each bed, were there for use instead of the outdoor privy. Carefully emptying these pots became one of Mary's many daily responsibilities.

Every Sunday, the family, with the exception of Mrs. Jacques, attended St. Paul's, the Anglican church in Innerkip, weather permitting. Not only was it difficult to lift her into the buggy, but she found the half-hour buggy

ride into town and back, very, very tiring. However, her church attendance was better in winter when her husband and sons could lift her into
the bob sleigh more easily. Somehow the sleigh ride seemed shorter. Mary
was rarely invited to join them for church. It was her job to stay home
and prepare the Sunday dinner.

The kitchen was large in comparison to the rest of the house and was
where the family spent most of their time. The old pine harvest table was
worn, yet had a great deal of character. Distress marks, black water rings
and gouges in the wood would indicate to even the most casual observer
that many meals had been served here. Six chairs of ash, elm or pine
flanked the table. Only two matched; the rest had come from various
places. As the Jacques family increased, so had the number of chairs at
their table. A stool at one end indicated there was a newcomer.

A rocker, Mrs. Jacques' chair, a washstand for Mrs. Jacques pitcher and
bowl and a small table were near the hearth surrounding the wood stove.
With the exception of a blue and yellow striped knit shawl on Mrs.
Jacques' chair, there was virtually no colour in the room. Mary's place
when she was not doing chores, was a small milk stool beside the butter
churn, near the end of the stove.

Kitchen utensils, pots and pans, compact barrels of salted meat and a
basket of potatoes were stored in the pantry beside the kitchen. Mary had
never heard of pickling until she came to live with the Jacques. Under Mrs.
Jacques' careful scrutiny she would stand at the table and wash and cut
quantities of green beans before storing them in brine-filled wooden barrels.
She also learned how to preserve fruit in sugar and make cider. The Jacques
enjoyed the homemade sweets, especially conserves, a candied fruit sometimes known as a sweetmeat. Like most of their neighbours, the Jacques had
a root cellar for storing vegetables in the side of the hill behind the house.
Often Mary would be sent there to fetch something for supper.

She peeled potatoes, prepared vegetables and set the table every night.
At supper time, she was allowed to sit with the family and permitted to
eat once everyone else had been served. As was the custom, grace was
said by Mr. Jacques before every meal. After supper Mary was expected
to clear the table, and wash and dry the dishes. She also did the family
mending in the evening while the others read or played board games after
their barn chores and any homework were finished.

Most of Mary's days were spent in the kitchen. Other than to dust and sweep, she was rarely in the other two rooms on the main floor, the parlour and the parents' bedroom. Originally, the bedroom had been a "borning room" where Mrs. Jacques delivered each of her seven children, and then it had become the family dining room. After she became ill, it had been converted to a bedroom. Mrs. Jacques hated to part with her dining room. It was considered a sign of affluence, but when she could no longer climb stairs, there had been no other choice. Lately, she felt she had little say in a lot of issues because of her health problems. This sense of powerlessness combined with daily pain fuelled her discontentment.

The upstairs was not spacious, just a couple of bedrooms and a small alcove. One room was Annie's, while the boys shared the larger one. The tiny space above the kitchen was where Mary slept.

Downstairs, the parlour was hardly ever used. Occasionally, Mrs. Jacques would do her needlework there, but that made it more difficult for her to scrutinize Mary's work in the kitchen. Special occasions like Christmas, a visit from the Rector or the arrival of unexpected guests might mean tea in the parlour. But because of Mrs. Jacques' condition, company was rarely invited. Both Annie and her mother wished they could afford a piano. The boys, however, were just as happy without it.

The first night Mary was in the kitchen cleaning up the supper dishes and sweeping the floor. It was almost eight o'clock and she was exhausted. Annie appeared and leaned casually in the doorway. She watched Mary for awhile before speaking.

"You must be glad that you finally got a place to live."

Mary, who was not only uncomfortable being watched but also somewhat guarded when dealing with Annie, said nothing and continued drying the dishes.

Annie moved toward her, grabbing the towel out of her hand. "Did you hear me, Girl?"

"Yes," Mary replied timidly, carefully setting a large dinner plate on the counter.

"Then answer me," she said, throwing the towel on the floor.

"Yes, I'm happy." Mary bent down, picked up the towel and continued drying the dishes.

"So what happened to your ma and pa?"

"Mama died and my papa lives in Scotland," Mary replied innocently. She was surprised that Annie cared.

"So how come you're not living with your pa?"

"I'm not sure. He just said this was best for me and my brothers and sisters."

"You have brothers and sisters?"

"I've got two brothers, Will and John, a big sister Carolyn and a baby sister. Her name is Emma," Mary replied sadly. That dreadful day at the Montreal dock momentarily flashed through her mind and was gone. She wiped away a tear with the tea towel.

Annie grinned. She liked to witness emotional situations, particularly those she'd created. Personal feelings were rarely discussed in the Jacques household.

"So where are they, these brothers and sisters?" she asked tauntingly. Her imposing height and intimidating presence seemed ominous to the little girl at the sink.

"I don't know," answered Mary, realizing now that Annie did not believe a word of what she had said. Quietly, she stacked the blue china cups in the cupboard. She noticed that there was only one without a chip.

"I'm sure you don't," Annie continued cynically. Annie had never felt close to her brothers, and it was difficult for her to comprehend that anyone could feel such closeness to a family. Annie's real reason for coming into the kitchen was to give Mary last minute instructions which her mother had forgotten earlier that day. Mary was to leave warm water in a basin for Mrs. Jacques in her bedroom every night at nine o'clock sharp. And she must have a clean towel right beside the basin.

As Mary began to absorb all these instructions, she wondered why everything had to be so exact, why time was so important and what would happen if she forgot something. Annie interrupted her thoughts.

"Girl, are you listening to me?"

"Yes," Mary replied.

"It's very important that you remember everything my mother needs.

Ever since she's been in that chair, we've had to look after her."

"That chair?"

"Yes, that chair, her wheelchair!"

"Wheelchair? You mean she doesn't get out of that chair?" Mary asked innocently.

"She hasn't been out of that chair for over a year except when Pa lifts her into bed at night or if she decides to go to church."

"She...she can't walk?" replied a stunned Mary.

"Why do you think you're here?" retorted Annie.

Mary was told very little about the Jacques family history and livelihood but over time she learned a great deal. Including an apple orchard, they had a hundred acre farm producing mainly grain and hay for their livestock which included horses, cattle, pigs and sometimes sheep. Each year as soon as the fields were dry enough, usually no later than mid-May, Mr. Jacques and his sons began planting the spring crops. Cultivating the land with horse-drawn implements and sowing the seeds were very time-consuming and demanded a great deal of physical labour. Luckily, Mr. Jacques was blessed with three sons who helped him in the fields. As he could not afford a seed drill, he had to borrow one if possible or rely on broadcasting the seed by hand. It was a tiresome job walking up and down the field, making large sweeping motions with his hand, dispensing the seed grain from the shallow wooden pan he carried with one hand. While it may have looked like a careless, random toss to an observer, in fact this was such a precise job that Mr. Jacques did it himself until he felt his sons were responsible enough to handle it. The seeds had to fall within the prepared soil; the field was then harrowed to ensure that soil would cover them. If poor weather damaged the seed, his crop would be ruined since he would not be able to buy new seed and replant in the same year.

Daniel Jacques was a lean, fine-boned man with an even disposition. He was not at all moody like his wife and, even in the years of crop failure, his personality remained unchanged. Not having attended school, he had never learned how to read. Nevertheless, Daniel believed that the *Farmer's Almanac* was the law and he relied on someone in his family to read it to him on a regular basis. For all his fifty-six years he had worked hard. Although he was a reasonably friendly man, he never had the luxury of free time for idle chatter. An honest man from working class stock, Daniel had known hard times. In the worst of those lean years he had been grateful to get someone's apple peelings.

He had married a woman twenty years younger than himself and within a time span of nine years was blessed with seven children. Parents welcomed big families since it meant more hands to do the work, especially on a farm. Unfortunately, in many families, a great number of young children succumbed to whooping cough, measles, diphtheria, polio, scarlet fever or rickets and died before their fifth birthday.

Three of the Jacques children never made it past the first year. Sarah and John died of diphtheria, and scarlet fever claimed Jacob's life. Four years after young Daniel's birth, their mother Mary Elizabeth, who went by the name May, fell seriously ill. She was only thirty. The doctors were unable to diagnose her sickness. At first they thought it was ague, a disease with flu-like symptoms as Mrs. Jacques did have a fever and chills, and she coughed relentlessly. She complained of shooting pains in her legs as well. As her condition deteriorated, the doctors knew that it was more serious than ague. It would be some time before Mr. Jacques learned that his wife's illness had many complexities. Not only did she suffer from a malingering affliction that caused her, over time, to become more and more physically debilitated, but she was also prone to sudden seizures and to frequent mild strokes. There was no cure in sight.

The broadcasting of seed as photographed by Reuben Sallows.
Courtesy Ontario Ministry of Agriculture and Food 179.69.108.

Mrs. Jacques was thirty-six when Mary came to stay. She had been confined to a wheelchair the previous year when the severity of her ailments caused almost total paralysis of both legs. She had very little mobility. May Jacques was an angry, bitter young woman, at times in a great deal of physical pain. Such continuous discomfort with no hope of relief would begin to explain her attitude in general and particularly her treatment of Mary. Unfortunately, Mary's seven-year-old mind could not have discerned such explanations.

By the last Sunday in June, Mary had been with the Jacques family for three weeks. A particularly nice day had prompted Mrs. Jacques' decision to go to church with the rest of her family. Mary did her chores quickly while they were gone. She did this so she could go for a short walk around the farm and explore her new surroundings.

The house, weathered a sombre shade of grey, was of old clapboard construction, nestled into the side of a small hill, facing south. The original house was quite small. An addition had been built at the back which became the kitchen and behind that, also attached, was the woodshed. The side door into the kitchen was the only entrance used. No-one ever went to the front of the house unless a photograph was being taken. Because of an overgrowth of poplars, chokecherries and golden rod by the side of the road, the house was partially hidden from view. Indeed, the Innerkip area was noted for its pretty, rolling countryside and abundance of trees.

Mary stepped gingerly outside the kitchen door and turned back to check the clock on the kitchen shelf, the only clock in the house. While she was not yet able to tell time, she knew that when it chimed twelve times, they would return. The big hand had to go completely around before that happened.

There was a slight overhang on the roof above the side door which created a small verandah. Mrs. Jacques favourite pastime was to sit here in her wheelchair and watch the road. In the barn were stored several old wicker chairs which the family would be getting out for the days of summer.

A group of elm and maple trees clustered together at the front of the house and, unless they were in full leaf, you could still see the road and anyone who might frequent it. Lilac bushes grew close to the house and gave a soft framing effect to an otherwise stark little grey dwelling.

Mary's curiosity did not lie with what was beyond the front of the house or down the road. Her interest was in the yard and the intrigues of the woods just beyond the barn, all places still a mystery to the young girl.

A photograph of the Jacques home taken in the early 1890s. Note the pump outside the entrance to the kitchen and the woodpile in the left background. Posing for the picture are Daniel Jr. with his two dogs, Annie standing just behind her mother May, and Daniel Sr. sitting in a chair by the front door. *Courtesy Joseph Jacques.*

As she walked around to the back, a scrawny mustard coloured cat of questionable beauty appeared from the barn and went right to Mary. As she knelt to pet it, the cat stretched its lanky body and rubbed its neck against her leg. Although she had little experience with animals, Mary gently picked it up and stroked its unkempt coat. She sensed an immediate friendship.

"Well, aren't you a sight!" Mary said as she stroked its back. The cat relaxed in her arms and began to purr. She continued to stroke gently. "I think you need a friend. Would you like to be my friend?" she asked politely. Without waiting for a response, she spoke again. "Then it's settled. We're friends." She set it down on the ground and started walking, the cat following along beside her.

By the time she reached the top of the hill, Mary was out of breath. The view was beautiful. The house below looked tiny, the barn and shed even smaller. Mary felt very big standing so high above everything as a slight breeze ruffled her brown pinafore and apron. Brushing a few strands of curly blonde hair out of her eyes, she continued on her little adventure.

To the west there was a dense thicket of trees and heavy ground cover. As she walked in this direction, the dry ground crunched under her thin worn shoes, brown oxford style cast-offs from the orphanage. She had stopped counting the knots in her laces. There were just too many.

Mary sat on an old stump and looked around. It was quiet except for a noisy robin somewhere in the distance. Mary picked up some interesting twigs and leaves and put them in her apron pocket. As her pockets were not very large, soon she had all she could carry.

Beyond the wooded area she caught a glimpse of tall grasses, scrub cedars and small pools of water full of cattails. This must be what the Jacques called the bogs. Mr. Jacques was forever telling the boys to stay away from them. Mary reminded herself of this warning, and of the time.

She turned eastward and began to head for home. Home: what a strange word. Was this really going to be her home? She wondered, would she ever think of this as home?

"Come on, Cat. It's time to go back," she spoke kindly to her new companion. It obeyed. Mary loved the out-of-doors and decided she would try to spend as much time here as she was allowed.

The sound of the approaching buggy wheels could be heard as she got near the house. The cat darted into the barn and Mary, running breathlessly into the kitchen, sat herself down on her perch by the stove.

Three

SETTLING IN

"No formal agreement has been entered into
between the home and those receiving the children
beyond signing the application form…and the foster-
parents see that they are not likely to be interfered
with if they overwork and otherwise take advantage
of their young charges."[7]

July 11, 1892

"WHAT ON earth are you doing with that corn broom? Have you no sense at all, Girl? Use the other one. It's far stronger and I don't want a slipshod job either. I want it done right and proper the first time!" Mrs. Jacques bellowed from her wheelchair across the room as she threw up her hands in a gesture of disgust.

"But you said I could use either, Ma'am," Mary replied shyly.

"I said no such thing. Now get on with your work and don't talk back, Girl."

Mary exchanged brooms and said nothing more. As she swept, the woman nattered away without seeming to want a response, just an audience.

"I can't run this household by myself, what with Annie working all day and the boys in the fields. I'm left to see that everything is managed properly. If I can't count on you, then what good are you?"

Having finished the floor by this time, Mary began to clear the breakfast table. Try as she might to ignore the woman, the words still hurt and Mary's eyes filled with tears. It was going to be a long, hot day.

"I have so much to do for tomorrow."

Mrs. Jacques was referring to the work bee that was to take place in her home at two o'clock the next day. Work bees, as they were called, had become very popular. The idea that "many hands make light work" had been a part of life since early pioneer days. A work bee could be organized for a variety of reasons: to shear sheep, erect a building, husk corn, pare apples for drying and, in Mrs. Jacques' case, to sew carpet rags.

At the moment, rag carpets could be found only in the Jacques' parlour, but Mrs. Jacques wanted them elsewhere as well. Such profusion was considered a sign of prosperity. Her nearest neighbours, Mrs. Graves and Mrs. McLaren, had accepted her invitation.

While the intention of work bees was to accomplish a job, they were also social gatherings. Country folks had little opportunity for visiting their neighbours, enjoying each other's company and dispensing the latest gossip. Not unlike Rachel Lynde who sojourned to Green Gables to inspect the "Anne" girl, the neighbours were curious about the "little immigrant" who had come to live with May and Daniel Jacques.

Mrs. Jacques nattered on, "I need you to get the rag boxes out of the loft. Put them in the front room. My sewing basket's in the bottom drawer of the jam cupboard. See that it's out as well."

As much as Mary did not look forward to extra chores, the thought of having someone besides Mrs. Jacques in the house was a pleasant one. She longed to hear voices and laughter from people even if they were strangers.

Mindlessly, she went through the daily routine her mistress had so carefully mapped out. Luckily, fetching water, sweeping and scrubbing the floor and washing dishes could all be done while her mind wandered.

Mary thought about Cat and wondered what it did all day in the barn. How she would love to have had the cat in the house with her. But she did not dare ask! In fact, she had not even mentioned it for fear somehow Mrs. Jacques would put an end to this pleasure. With a smile on her face, she imagined how wonderful it would be to curl up with Cat beside her

The vegetable garden was an important source of supply for the farm kitchen. Caring for the fledgling plants would be a chore assigned to one of the younger children. This young boy, obviously a good worker, may have resembled Daniel Jr. *Courtesy Barry Hoskins, Heritage Cards.*

on her cot in the loft, and fall asleep next to its gentle purring.

"I don't know what you're so happy about." Mrs. Jacques sharp tongue brought Mary back to her dishwashing chore with a sudden jolt. "There's so much to be done. I want the grey rug in the hall taken outside and swept after your regular chores are done. I expect my home to look proper for my guests."

"It was done on Tuesday, Ma'am," Mary interjected, speaking for the second time in over an hour.

"And it will be done again today."

Mary was getting discouraged. The weather was warm and the sunshine inviting. She had hoped to get her work done by mid-afternoon so she would have a little free time before preparing supper. But with extra jobs to do, this was not likely to happen.

Finally, she was finished and allowed to go outside. Her favourite game was to take her rubber ball, which she carried in her apron pocket, and bounce it on the far side of the house against the hard clapboard, as far away as possible from Mrs. Jacques' hearing. She invented little challenges like trying to catch it with her left hand or pop it directly in her apron pocket.

Within a few minutes, Daniel Jr., the youngest in the family, appeared at the side of the house. "Would you like to play?" Mary asked.

"Why not," he shrugged. They threw the ball back and forth and laughed whenever one of them missed. Daniel was obviously much better at catching and throwing but showed a reasonable amount of patience with Mary. For a little while she forgot her loneliness and began to act like a seven-year-old child.

"And what do you think Mother will say about this, Daniel?"The laughter came to an abrupt halt. "Playing with a girl and the help at that!" The words came from his sister's lips. Annie's harsh manner intimidated both of them.

With that, Daniel threw Mary's ball as hard as he could into the thicket of trees at the top of the hill and darted around the corner in the direction of the barn. Annie's mission had been accomplished and she walked back toward the house, thinking about Mary. In Annie's mind, Mary was different. Her clothes were not as nice as hers and she spoke with a slight accent. Mary was not part of her family and never would be. She was a servant girl, needed here on the

A formal studio photograph of May Jacques with her daughter Annie, circa 1893. *Courtesy Joseph Jacques.*

farm to help her invalid mother. Her brother should not play with a servant—it wasn't proper.

Mary raced to the top of the hill in an attempt to find her one and only toy. In a frantic search, she dropped down an all fours, unaware that she was staining the front of her apron. Her tears were not only for the lost ball but also because of her disappointment in Daniel. She thought he was going to be her friend.

Annie's voice, calling her back to the house, interrupted her search. It was time to prepare supper and bake for tomorrow's company.

Daniel avoided looking at Mary at the supper table and nothing was said about the incident. Mary truly believed that he was sorry. She, however, was reprimanded for getting her apron dirty, but Mary had anticipated the scolding. With all that had happened that day, a few more harsh words did not make any difference.

Mrs. Jacques admitted to being unusually fatigued that evening and introduced Mary to yet another task. "When I'm tired like this, I like to have
my hair combed," she said. Her dark, thick straight hair was coiled on top
of her head in a bun. She removed several hairpins and the long, black
mane fell halfway down her back. It became Mary's job to comb and brush
her hair until Mrs. Jacques felt satisfied.

And so she sat in her wheelchair by the stove and Mary stood behind
her and brushed and combed, sometimes for as long as an hour, while the
others pursued their own activities. Frequently, Mr. Jacques went to the
barn since smoking was not allowed in the house.

"I'll let you know when you may stop."

Mary's arms ached and if she slowed down she would be reminded of
her job. "I can't feel it. Press harder with the comb or there's no point in
doing it."

When she was finally given permission to go to bed, Mary was relieved
to be alone in her little loft. She longed to hold the barn cat in her arms
and fell asleep dreaming about Cat.

*Mary found the rhythmic purr of her feline friend soothing. The cat bur-
rowed further under her bent elbow and finally rested its head on her chest.
The soft little belly rose and fell as it drifted off to sleep.*

*Suddenly and without warning, the cat sprang to life and jumped off her
body. She had forgotten where she was, of course, the hayloft. The sun was beaming in through open boards. It was far too glorious a day to waste sleeping.*

*"You're so smart," she said, peering over the loft at a pair of big green eyes
staring up at her. "We should be out in the sun, not stuck here in this loft."
Mary ran to the ladder and climbed down. She slowly pulled the barn door
open and before she could step out, the cat slid past her and was gone, moving so fast that Mary was even uncertain as to which direction it had gone.*

*Her instinct told her the cat probably headed for the grove of trees beyond
Mama's clothesline. She ran up the small hill, half expecting to see Will and John
playing ball in the clearing but they weren't there. And neither was the cat.*

*"Cat, where did you go? I know you're hiding. Come on out, Cat, wherever
you are."*

*She was getting annoyed. "Let's go back to the house. Mama might have a
treat for us." Cat loved Mama's treats, fresh cream or bread and honey. She*

heard a sound, thought she saw something and reached out to grab it. "Now I've got you," she laughed.

Mary opened her eyes. It was dark. She saw nothing. There was no hill, no clothesline, no Cat and no Mama. She was alone in her little loft. Mary curled up in a ball in the darkness and softly cried herself to sleep.

Four

THE WORK BEE

"As a rule, the homes in which the children are
placed in Canada are not so selected, and it is very
certain that great abuses do ensue."[8]

July 12, 1892

THE NEXT morning Mrs. Jacques waited and watched anxiously at the
window. Everything was in apple-pie order; she had seen to that. Finally, she
turned away and made herself busy sorting some of the rags she had saved
for the sewing bee. After all, she believed that "a watched pot never boils."

Her tension eased when she heard a knock at the door promptly at two.

"Girl, go and greet my guests and be quick about it. I don't want them
waiting," she ordered.

"Yes, Ma'am." Mary ran to open the door. But it was not either of the
neighbours they were expecting. There stood a little old man, bent over,
wearing dark, dusty, thread-bare clothes. Mary looked down. He had
holes in both his boots. Tied to a tree nearby was a skinny grey mare,
weighted down with bundles and saddle bags.

"Is the missus at home?" he asked.

Mary was silent, not knowing what to make of him. By now, Mrs.
Jacques had wheeled herself to the door, disappointed not to hear the
voices of her company yet curious to know who had come calling.

When the pedlar saw that she was in a wheelchair, he quickly untied his horse and moved it closer to the door for her inspection. "Have a look at my wares. I've pots and pans, lanterns, spices from the East and tonics to cure everything from corns to stomach ailments, catarrh and ague," he announced.

Mrs. Jacques took a quick look, for she was a curious woman. She picked up a small round pan made of tin, poor man's silver, then handed it back. "I've better of my own," she retorted.

"Have you some knives to be sharpened or scissors to point for a bit of spare change," he replied quickly.

"I don't need anything sharpened. You best be on your way," she said firmly, wanting him to leave before her company arrived. It would not look good if her friends realized she could not afford to buy anything.

"Have you at least got a piece of bread or cheese for a hungry traveller?" he asked with some hesitation in his voice.

"Be on your way. I've no time for beggars." Waving him off, she turned away. Mary stood at the window and watched.

"Close the door, Girl. I've no use for higgling and haggling. I hope we've seen the last of him."

Mary felt sorry for the old man and wished she could have given him something to eat. He was just out of sight when Mrs. Graves, along with her ten-year-old daughter, Martha, came down the lane in their horse and buggy.

With Mary's help, they carried in several wicker baskets of rags. When she saw the little girl, Mary was hopeful that she might have a playmate for the afternoon. Soon afterwards, Mrs. McLaren was dropped off by her husband en route to town for supplies. Annie joined the group as well, having stayed home from work to be part of this social event. Her mother made no mention of the travelling pedlar either to her or to the guests.

Once all were settled in the parlour, it was Mary's job to serve tea and the biscuits she had baked the previous day. She was eager to meet the neighbours.

"Ladies, this is Mary, the new girl I told you about," Mrs. Jacques announced with a sweep of her hand. Mary smiled and nodded her head. It was the first time that Mrs. Jacques had referred to her by name.

Mrs. McLaren seemed particularly interested in Mary. "How old are you,

When a lady went visiting or "calling" she wore a long flowing skirt with a fitted high-necked blouse and a jacket. The more elaborate the hat, the more fashionable and prosperous she was considered to be. The photograph is of Mabel McDougall Hewson, paternal grandmother of Mary Pettit, circa 1908. *Courtesy the Pettit Collection.*

dear?" she asked as she adjusted her glasses and took a better look.

"I'll be eight years old on August 2," Mary replied proudly. She was anxious to tell someone her birthday was close at hand. Mrs. Graves turned to Mrs. Jacques as if Mary were either deaf or invisible. "She's awful scrawny and thin, May. Will she be strong enough to be of help to you?"

"There wasn't a lot of choice in younger girls. It was the best we could do," Mrs. Jacques replied.

Mary tried to ignore the conversation but the words ran through her head over and over, "the best we could do." Once tea was served, she was allowed to go outside, for it was obvious she did not belong. Annie was sitting over in one corner, laughing and chatting with Martha. As she walked out of the room, Mrs. Jacques reminded her to watch her "Ps and Qs." Mary headed straight for the barn to look for Cat, glad to escape outside into the sunshine.

For the next week, Mary hunted for her rubber ball every opportunity she had. But she never found it. Finally in desperation, she made a new ball by tying tiny rag scraps together, leftovers from the work bee. It was not nearly as good as the rubber one but better than nothing.

Mary realized that she would never have thought of this idea if it had not been for Mrs. Jacques' little get together. So something good did come from the work bee after all.

Five

MARY'S BIRTHDAY

"In many cases the children were totally unprepared
and unsuited for the work demanded of them and
too often there was little or no inspection of their
situations once they were placed."[9]

August 2, 1892

WHEN MARY woke up at six o'clock, not a cloud was in the sky. It looked
like a perfectly beautiful day. She hoped something exciting would happen
on her birthday.

Mrs. Jacques was aware that it was a special day for Mary, but said nothing. Mary went through her daily routine of household chores, hoping that
at least it might be acknowledged. Birthdays up to this point had held little
significance to Mary. She had little memory of the first four and, after that,
her life had been in such a turmoil that birthdays had been forgotten. Mary
had hoped that there might be a small celebration for this one. Since she
had moved in two months ago, she had been dropping hints, making com-
ments that were not particularly subtle but typical of a young child. She
wanted to make sure that everyone knew her birthday was close at hand.

"I can carry that all my myself. You know I'm almost eight...Some
people think I'm only six because I'm small but did you know I'll be eight
in August?...I think it would be exciting to have a birthday cake...Annie,

Mary Jacques, granddaughter of Daniel with the Jacques home in the background. Note the dinner bell on a pole. Mary would have rung this bell to call the men in from the field at meal times or whenever she might need help if Mrs. Jacques was suffering from a seizure. *Courtesy Joseph Jacques.*

could you read when you were eight years old?" Most of the time she was ignored or reminded to get back to work.

By early afternoon Mary had finished the lunch dishes and was about to dust the parlour. "You can leave the dusting for today, seeing that it's your birthday and all. Go on out and play." Mrs. Jacques shooed her to the door with her hand as she uttered these surprising, and almost more than hoped for words.

She ran to the door with enthusiasm but turned back and said, "Thank you, Ma'am, for remembering."

"I still expect you to peel potatoes and scrub carrots for dinner. Now run along."

"Yes, Ma'am," Mary replied excitedly.

She ran to the barn and climbed the ladder to the hayloft. There she found her friend asleep on the straw-covered floor and she exuberantly scooped the cat into her arms. "Cat, wake up, this is a very special day! Do you know why? Of course you do, silly. It's my birthday." While she spoke, she climbed carefully down the ladder, holding Cat tightly with one arm and ran out into the sunshine.

She plunked her friend on the ground and they went for their usual walk across the fields and following the rail fence to the top of the hill

A snake rail fence, one style of early Canadian cedar rail fences. *Illustration by C. W. Jeffries. From* **Fences.**

behind the barn while Mary chattered away. One would almost think the cat understood her, although the conversation was a bit one-sided.

Mary filled her apron pockets with collectibles. These treasures always found their way into her little bedroom in the loft. By now she had accumulated an assortment of leaves, rocks, twigs and several multi-coloured agates which she had squirrelled away in a faded red tea caddy, a rather unexpected surprise found buried in the hay loft a few weeks earlier. Mary had been disappointed to find it empty, but still it was a pretty little box. She hid it under her cot for fear someone would discover it and take it away from her.

The day had an unusual ending. While the Jacques were finishing dinner, Annie presented her with a birthday present, an old primer reader which she claimed she had read at Mary's age. "You wanted to know if I could read when I was eight. This is what I read," Annie announced proudly at the dinner table and handed the book to the birthday girl. Mary was grateful for the gift. Not until later by the light of the moon in her tiny loft did she realize that the words were "too big."

Mr. Jacques gave Mary a piece of real chocolate. She was thrilled. Only once before had she eaten chocolate and that was one Christmas at the orphanage. "You're a hard worker and a good girl, Mary," he said with a smile. Mary cherished those words for he was a quiet man and rarely spoke to her.

She was happy as she climbed the stairs to go to bed. She knew Cat would be delighted to share her chocolate. What she did not know was that a little blue rubber ball was lying on her pillow.

Six

SCHOOL DAYS

"For most immigrant children the school was a
world away, and if they entered it at all, it was for a
brief and fleeting time, too brief to learn much, but
long enough to feel the hurt of being looked upon as
a ragamuffin with a funny accent."[10]

September 15, 1892

THAT AUTUMN brought new hope to the Jacques family when their
eldest boy, sixteen-year-old Thomas, got a job working at the gristmill.

Gristmills were scattered across the country, set adjacent to a river or
spillway to supply the necessary water power. Often they were built just
at the edge of town.

These mills were extremely important to the growth of a community.
A local mill meant that people no longer had to grind their own grain
into flour, a very time-consuming and laborious task, or to transport their
grain long distances to the nearest mill. Since bread was a staple food,
flour was an essential commodity.

Innerkip was no exception. Their gristmill had been built at the edge
of the village in 1877 by Robert K. Thomson and Thomas Frederick
Mitchell, and the river dammed to make a millpond. A three-storey-high
stone building, it was the tallest in the village. The mill had changed hands

several times until it was sold to Charles Press and John E. Hewitt sometime in the 1880s. After Hewitt sold his shares to Charles Press the following November, Press was the sole owner of the mill.

The miller was expected to give his customers good service. Farmers
wanted top quality flour, even if their wheat might not be the best. They
also expected a good volume of flour in proportion to the quality of
wheat. "A competent miller in the mid-1800s had to be able to produce
one (196 lb.) barrel of superfine flour from no more than 4½ bushels of
wheat (60 lbs. to the barrel)."[11]

In some cases, the farmer supervised his grain being milled, often to
ensure they were getting full measure. Charles Press discouraged this
practice and tried to divert their attention to other tasks that might need
to be done while they were this close to town. He was well-known for
his quick, efficient service and it always took more time if the farmer was
present. As with every business, the miller's best source of advertising
was a satisfied customer.

A good miller like Charles Press chose his employees carefully. The
work day was long and strenuous and there was also an element of danger.
Pests, fire, floods and accidents could shut a mill down in a matter of
hours.

It was Thomas' dream to apprentice at the mill. He knew it would take
a long time and he must start by doing simple tasks. But he was a quiet,
determined boy with a great deal of patience. Initially he was hired to
sweep, unload wagons, hitch-up horses and look after the mill cats, kept
to control the mice. Charles knew that Thomas Jacques was an intelligent
boy, who would work hard and follow orders to the letter. These were
important qualities for a miller's apprentice. He also hoped Thomas
would become his successor, since he had no children of his own. The boy
was grateful for the opportunity, and the Jacques were relieved that now
two of their children had jobs.

Chris and Daniel were returning to school. Blandford School S. S. No.
3, which Mary thought sounded like an uninteresting name for a school,
was on the corner of the 8th concession and a county road named East-
wood Side Road. It had opened in 1866 after it became obvious that more
accommodation was needed than the 18th line Union School could offer.
As a result of dissension among the trustees, the north families went to

Ratho School, between the 11th and 13th concessions, and the village families held school at Vincent's Hall, on Vincent Street in town. After a year of verbal battles, the Union Section split and each built a school. Thus, the name Blandford School S. S. No. 3 had significance for the trustees if not for the children.

While legislation to initiate taxation for school funding had begun in the late eighteen-forties,[12] individual families contributed to the funding of the school. Varying sums of money were paid to help cover the school-teacher's wage, the amount being determined by the number of children in the family attending school. This cost may have been one of the reasons why the Jacques chose not to send Mary to school on a regular basis.

The schoolteacher often received a very small salary for his or her services, but was expected to do much more than just teach. It was the teacher's responsibility to exemplify the moral behaviors that the children read about in their school books. The teacher must exhibit patience, kindness and tolerance and set a good example for the students at all times. Drinking alcohol and rowdiness were frowned upon and regular church attendance was expected. Teachers enforced strict discipline in the school; in most cases order was maintained by a liberal use of the "birch rod" or "blue beech."[13] The only subjects taught were reading, writing and arithmetic as many teachers had little knowledge and expertise in other areas. Often the teacher would take room and board with a family living near the school.

Blandford School was almost two miles from the Jacques farm and harsh winters often made it very difficult, if not impossible, to get there. They had to leave no later than 7:30 a.m. in order to arrive on time, for Miss McGuire, the teacher, had no use for tardiness. In the winter it meant leaving the house when it was still dark. Although Mary left at the same time as the boys, she did not always arrive at the same time. Mrs. Jacques told her never to cross fences or take short cuts and never to accept a lift from a neighbour. The boys did as they wished.

The morning of September 15 was Mary's first day at school. Unfortunately all the other children had started the week before and were nicely settled in, but Mrs. Jacques had insisted that she needed Mary at home a little longer. And so, on this special Monday morning that Mary had waited so patiently for, she started out with the boys but soon lagged behind. From a distance she could see a large school bell on top of the cedar shingled roof. Clutching her old leather satchel with a broken strap, Annie's castoff, Mary arrived, breathless and filled with nervous anxiety. Blandford School No. 3 turned out to be a small, grey fieldstone building with two doors, one marked "Boys," the other "Girls."

Mary had waited and so looked forward to the arrival of this day, but now that it was here she felt panicky and unsure of herself. Her hands were sweaty and her heart raced. Knowing that most of the children would have started school a year before her, she was afraid she would be far behind the others of her age.

She began walking more slowly, and then stopped a safe distance from the schoolyard. Taking a big breath, she studied her surroundings. East of the school were the woods and the Thames River. It was here that the children spent their noon hour playing among the willow and apple trees that banked the river. On her first day of school Mary decided that S. S. #3 should have been called Willowcreek School. She soon learned that both the teacher's switches and the children's whistles came from these willows.

There was one birch tree with a limb hanging low over the riverbank. Joey Skillings had tied a rope to it, making the most wonderful swing for those who dared to dangle just inches above the water. On either side of the riverbank, the ground, in the spring, would be peppered with violets, wild strawberries and jack-in-the-pulpits. This time of year, however, goldenrod, wild aster and Queen Anne's lace lined the banks.

The little stone schoolhouse was nestled quietly beside a grove of apple trees with a small clearing on one side where a group of girls, squealing with delight, were playing "Duck, duck, goose." Mary moved a little closer. It was obvious her brown dress, made of linsey-woolsey and covered by a grey pinafore for protection against stains, was shabby and plain compared to the flowered print dresses and matching bonnets of the other girls. She sat under an apple tree and waited and watched the girls at play in the schoolyard. Beyond, she could see other small groups along the edge of the river.

The school bell rang and the children lined up at their respective doors.

Responding to a nod from the teacher, the children began to file in, one by one. Mary followed behind the last girl. The teacher, with her long sweeping skirt and crisp white high collared blouse, greeted her at the door. She was a woman in her early twenties, slender and petite, about five feet tall, with chestnut brown hair neatly secured in a bun. Mary thought she was beautiful.

"Good morning, young lady. I'm Miss McGuire, and what is your name?"

"Good morning, Ma'am. I'm Mary."

"And your family name?"

Mary paused for a moment. "Jacques," she replied softly after biting her bottom lip.

"No, it ain't," interjected Billy Skillings, a red-headed freckle-faced boy of about ten. The rest of the children were putting their belongings on their hooks but suddenly became very quiet. "She's the little orphan who come to stay at the Jacques' place. She ain't no real Jacques." Mary searched the group of eyes staring at her, hoping Chris or Dan would come to the rescue. She spotted both of them. They were silent. Mary realized that her friendship with Dan was strictly limited to playing together on the farm when he had no-one else. Her eyes dropped to the floor.

"Welcome to our school, Mary," the teacher replied without hesitating, smiling as she placed her arm gently around Mary's shoulders and encouraged her to come inside.

"Boys and girls, please take your places and prepare for morning devotions. Mary, this can be your hook." Miss McGuire turned and pointed to one of the lower hooks that lined the back wall. A variety of caps, dinner pails and satchels were already there. Mary put her satchel, Annie's cast-off, on the hook by its good strap. It dangled precariously and easily stood out from the others, just like Mary did.

"Come and sit beside Laura. You can share her reader. I'm sure the two of you will get along just fine." The teacher smiled in a maternal way before she turned to her class and resumed a serious, dignified look. Mary sat down beside her. Laura appeared happy to have a new friend, but then turned away as though embarrassed. Mary would have liked to reach out and touch the pretty red ribbons on Laura's long, dark braids that fell halfway down her back.

The School Act of 1871 provided the initial legislation towards compulsory education, yet many pupils attended in a highly irregular fashion. Note the stove in
this typical one room school. Mary's school would have resembled this room.
George M. Douglas Collection, courtesy Katharine Hooke.

"Boys and girls, let us begin with the Lord's Prayer," Miss McGuire said
with an officious voice. Everyone stood up. Mary got out of her seat a
moment after the others. She had heard the Lord's Prayer many times at
the orphanage and Sheltering Home and had memorized it diligently, like
all the other orphans. But even though the words were familiar, it sounded
strange to hear it being recited by the students in this little one-room
schoolhouse. As the morning routines got underway, Mary began to grow
more comfortable in her new surroundings. She was eager to learn, anxious to please and desperately wanted to fit in with the others.

There were three rows of double desks facing the blackboard in the
schoolhouse. Natural light was used whenever possible. The students sat
on hard, wooden benches without backs. These benches were all the same
height in order to accommodate the older students. This meant the
younger ones dangled their feet in the air. Mary, small for her age, was
not able to touch the floor. She hoped that it would go unnoticed.

The younger children, on one side of the room, worked with slate pencils on their slate boards. The older students used quill pens, ink and paper.

Towards the back, in the centre of the room, was the stove with its great stovepipe running the length of the room, providing additional heat in the cold winter months. A stack of wood was at the back of the room and, beside it, a pile of kindling. In the colder months the older students were assigned the task of starting a fire in the stove before school began. Finding firewood was never a problem since the area had abundant trees and usually parents would provide split wood. Gathering wood, especially kindling from fallen branches was considered a "fun" job and occasionally meant recess was a little longer than usual.

The teacher's desk was at the front of the room on a slightly raised platform. There were three two-paned windows on either side of the school. In one corner was a pail and dipper. Each school day a student was appointed to fill the pail with fresh water from the pump outside. Mary thought this would be a fine job, even though it was something she did for Mrs. Jacques daily. Here, since everyone did it, it meant she belonged.

The very first time she was the "water girl" she mentioned it to Mrs. Jacques so she would realize it was important for Mary not to miss school. But the very next morning Mrs. Jacques wasn't feeling "up-to-snuff" and refused to let Mary go. Although the teacher was understanding about her absence, Mary felt she had let Miss McGuire down. She never mentioned her job at school to Mrs. Jacques again. Very quickly Mary learned that she could only confide in certain people.

Mary loved everything about school. She shared a desk, had her very own hook and for the most part was treated equally, thanks to Miss McGuire. By now she had been at school a couple of weeks and this particular afternoon the class seemed restless. Against her better judgement, the teacher let them play "twenty questions." One student would think of a specific word representing a person, place or thing and the others tried to guess who or what it was by asking up to twenty questions that could only be answered "yes" or "no."

Joe Skillings, a senior, was asked to begin. A tall, thin curly-headed boy, and a very good student, he smiled, took his place at the front of the room and nodded when he was ready. That was the cue for the students, one by one, to begin asking him questions.

"Is it a toy?"

"No."

"Is it an animal?"

"No."

"Is it a person?"

"Yes."

"Is it a boy?"

"No."

"Is it a girl?" There was a burst of laughter in the classroom, for the question, asked by six-year-old Martha Preston, was ridiculous. What else could it be?

"Yes," was Joe's answer.

"Is she in the room?"

"Yes."

"Is it the new girl?"

"Yes."

"Is it Mary?" At this point heads were turning toward Mary and she blushed. She was not used to such attention.

"No."

The students looked confused since there was only one new girl and that was Mary. The teacher interjected.

"Joe, is your word Mary?" she asked patiently.

"No, Miss McGuire, it's orphan!" he replied boldly. The children laughed. Deeply embarrassed, Mary tried to hold back her tears. She did not know what to do. Miss McGuire told Joe to remain after the others were dismissed at the end of the day and then calmly asked everyone to open their readers.

The teacher pondered the type of punishment she should administer. Usually she had her students write out lines, sit in the corner wearing the dunce cap or sit beside a student of the opposite sex. But in this case, it was different. Joe was a senior, which meant he was to set a good example for the younger children. He was a bright boy and knew better. What he did was cruel and hurtful. There was only one thing to do.

At three-thirty sharp the rest of the students were dismissed and sent on their way. Miss McGuire picked up the willow switch that was in one

Toys for young children were few and usually homemade. Young children in the country often had only their siblings for company. Josie Chesney, Mary's friend at school, could have looked much like this young girl, shown here with her wagon and her dog. *Barry Hoskins, Heritage Cards.*

corner of the little schoolroom. It leaned against the wall as a reminder to the children that misbehaviour would not be tolerated. Under Miss McGuire's care it had never been used in the two years she had been at Blandford School S. S. #3.

She turned toward Joe and said, "Let this be a reminder never to speak in such a way to deliberately hurt another student in my class. Hold out both your hands." She strapped him five times on each hand. Joe held back tears until he was well on his way home. He hoped that his younger brother Billy would not mention this to his father or he would probably incur another switching when he arrived home.

It was a difficult decision for a young teacher to make, but it was the right one. She never heard the word from her pupils again.

Joe's humiliation of Mary proved to be an isolated incident. The weeks slipped past quickly and it was soon forgotten by the children. Mary was a happy little girl when she was at school and in a short period of time she had lots of friends. For her, most learning came easily. At first, reading was a bit of a struggle, but all of a sudden it just seemed to make sense and she was on her way. When she graduated to the Second Reader, Mary was thrilled. Now she could have her very own goose pen and homemade ink.

Cursive writing was a highly prized skill. The children had to line their own paper and practise the "slants" and "curves" to form the letters perfectly. Mary struggled with this as her small hands lacked co-ordination and strength. "Take your time, Mary. It's hard to rule your page at first, but neatness is very important." It seemed that tardiness and sloppiness were the worst sins at school.

Mary especially loved to bring her writing home so she could share it with her barnyard friend. Sitting in the loft with Cat, her skinny little legs dangling over the edge, she would clear her throat and read the words that she had diligently copied and read aloud in unison with the rest of the children at school. "Perseverance overcomes difficulties." Mary would end with a smile. She did not always understand what she wrote but knew that Miss McGuire was teaching good things. All lessons taught in school had moralistic overtones in an attempt to develop gratitude and humility. Parents were judged by the way their children behaved; even the very young were expected to act like "little" adults.

School was a place to work, not play, but every Friday afternoon they had a spell-down or what some called a "spelling bee." Two teams were picked, and the children took turns spelling words read aloud by the teacher. Each time a word was misspelled, that student had to sit down. The last child standing was the winner, and somewhat of a celebrity until the next week when he or she had their position challenged.

Mary never hoped to win, but as her reading improved, so did her spelling. Once she came close, but the dismissal bell rang and Miss McGuire declared a tie between Mary and Jenny Allenby. Josephine Chesney, better known as Josie, leaned over and whispered, "Everybody knows you're a better speller than Jenny. And she started school a year before you."

Mary learned a great deal at school besides the three Rs. She learned the value of friendship and loyalty. On her first day Josie had given her some good advice. "Never ever go to the privy by yourself, Mary. You'll be sorry if you do!" she added emphatically. "The boys think it's a great sport to hang over the top and peek through the slats to catch a glimpse of you going to the bathroom."

"Why would they do that?"

"Who knows? Just remember to take a buddy, someone you trust to stand guard at the door."

"Does everybody do that?"

"Girls do for sure, boys don't give two hoots."

"That's so dumb," Mary added.

"Boys are dumb. There isn't any boy I can think of that doesn't like to play a trick, and the meaner, the better. It gives me goose bumps when I think of what Billy and Joe Skillings did to my brother last spring."

"Which brother?"

"Jimmy, the *best ball player in the world*," she said proudly, and then added, "which is why they did it."

"Did what?"

"They put an old board across the latch on the privy door and wouldn't let him out."

"What's that got to do with playing ball?"

"Everything. The Skillings wanted to win the Blandford School championship, but with Jimmy on the other team, they didn't stand a chance." Some years the teams were as small as four or five players, but Blandford School always tried to have two teams, to instill enthusiasm and create competition. Sometimes an event was planned with Ratho School to the north, but travelling between schools was difficult and hard to organize.

"Didn't anyone miss him?"

"Yeah, we all did. Joe said Jimmy had a toothache, ran home to get some medicine and would try to get back for the game. That sounded like something Jimmy would do and not tell anyone. Even Miss McGuire believed the story. So they started the game without him and Jimmy's team was losing. All of a sudden he appeared looking real mad."

"How'd he get out?"

"Somebody on his own team went to use the privy and heard him shouting. If it hadn't been so far away, we all would have heard him."

"What happened to the boys?"

Miss McGuire wouldn't let them play the rest of the game and Jimmy's team won 18-16." Josie grinned, showing all her teeth.

Baseball was growing in popularity. For many young rural boys, becoming a top-notch ball player would be a dream come true. *Barry Hoskins, Heritage Cards.*

It did not take long before Mary got to know who could be trusted. Billy Skillings was not one of them. He was well-known for putting grasshoppers, frogs, spiders or parts of them in a young girl's lunch pail or pencil box. The shriller the scream, the more successful the prank.

Mary would never forget the morning Allan Fenlon dumped a bottle of water, used to clean slates, on Jenny Allenby's seat, while she was at the front reciting her three times table. Jenny, wearing a beautiful white pinafore and matching dress, was very fussy about her appearance. When she sat down, she let out a shriek as if she had seen a ghost. All of the children laughed. Not only did the wet seat surprise her, but the water was ice cold. Jenny jumped up, and all the children could see her pantaloons through her wet dress and petticoats. She ran out of the schoolroom, the teacher close at her heels.

The rest of the day Jenny wore a pair of breeches that had been left at school. They were two sizes too short, not to mention the fact that only boys wore them. Allan had to write out one hundred times in his best cursive handwriting, "I will not be mean to girls," and he had to sit beside Jenny one whole day. Mary was not sure if that was a fair punishment since Jenny hated him just as much as he hated her.

Spitballs thrown across the room when the teacher's back was turned, braids dipped into ink wells, notes passed and shoelaces tied together were all part of Mary's schooling at S. S. #3. But despite all, a fair bit of "learning" did take place.

She continued to sit beside Laura for the duration of the school year, but there were many days when her seat would be empty. Mrs. Jacques did not like to be alone; prior to Mary's arrival, a series of nurses had lived at the Jacques home. But Mrs. Jacques was a jealous woman and afraid their interests centred around her husband. She felt much safer with a young girl like Mary in the house, but resented how happy Mary was when she arrived home from school. Mary began to see a pattern to her absenteeism and she soon learned to be less animated in front of Mrs. Jacques. Unfortunately, the slightest change in Mary's personality would arouse Mrs. Jacques' suspicion.

"Well, you look like you have a bee in your bonnet! What's your problem, Girl?" Mrs. Jacques asked one day after Mary arrived home from school. For that matter Mary was purposely trying not to look too happy or too sad, but Mrs. Jacques seemed pleased with herself that she had made a discovery.

Mary was careful not to discuss school with her; she had learned that lesson only too well. If Mary was anticipating a special event, Mrs. Jacques would find out when it was, usually from one of her sons, and make sure she kept her home. If there was something that Mary dreaded, like a grammar test or public speaking, she'd make certain she went to school that day.

Mary replied cautiously, lowering her head to avoid eye contact. "Oh, nothing really, Ma'am. I had a special agate in my pocket...uh, it was a beautiful rainbow colour," she paused, wondering how much information she should provide, "and I lost it on my way home." Mary stopped, slowly raising her head and looked directly at the woman's face for a reaction.

Mrs. Jacques threw up one hand with disgust. It was not what she had expected. "That's utter foolishness. I've heard enough." Flicking her raised hand toward the door she said, "Now get on with your chores and spend your time worrying about more important things."

"Yes, Ma'am," Mary replied and ran to the chimney cupboard for her old clothes. One hand remained in her apron pocket tightly holding the rainbow-coloured agate that Josie, her new friend at school had given her that morning.

The story she had made up for Mrs. Jacques, her little tale of woe, was the only thing she could think of on the spur of the moment. She had hoped it would satisfy the woman's curiosity. This time it worked.

Seven

CAT GETS A NAME

"The society in which these youngsters were about to
begin their lives as Canadians, did not dislike children,
but in its treatment of them—especially those who
were the offspring of unknown and distant parents—it
seemed bent on thwarting any sense of self they may
have had, any tendency to feel special worth...not so
much out of villainy as out of morality, convinced that
the dampening of a child's spirit and the curbing of a
child's will by discipline were the obligations laid
upon it by a religious tradition."[14]

October, 1892

MARY DEVELOPED many friendships that first year at school, but the
girl who stole her heart was Josie. This little red-headed girl was only
seven but reading in the Second Reader like Mary. With six brothers and
sisters, Josie was congenial and helped out a lot at home, but rarely was
on the receiving end of attention herself. She needed a best friend almost
as badly as Mary did.

Gradually, Mary told her some of the details concerning her family in
Scotland and how they came to be separated. She had never confided in anyone before but felt she could trust her. While Mary did not dwell on the

painful memories of separation, Josie could tell it upset her to talk about this part of her past. She could not imagine having to live apart from her family.

Mary explained how Mr. Jacques had come to Stratford for a girl and she had been chosen. Josie knew the younger Jacques boys from school, but Annie and Thomas were too old for her to have even met. Mary told her about discovering Cat in the barn and how the animal had become her pet.

"What's the cat's name?" Josie asked innocently.

"He doesn't really have a name…Cat, I guess. That's all I've ever called him."

"Cat…that's awful. That's not a name. That's what he is. How'd you like to be called Girl?" Josie asked her.

"Mrs. Jacques calls me that all the time and I hate it. You've got a point Jos. I should give him a name. But what?"

"What's he look like?"

"Oh, he's beautiful. He's sorta long and thin and he's kinda yellow. Well, not exactly yellow, kinda dark yellow."

"What's he remind you of?"

"Nothing really, well, maybe mustard. Yeah, he looks like mustard."

"There you go. You've just named him. If he reminds you of mustard, why not call him that. It's better than Cat, that's for sure."

"I could try it and see if he likes that name." Mary pondered the idea for a moment. "You wouldn't believe the sound he makes when you hold him and pet him. His purr is so loud. I'm sure the Edwards a mile down the road can hear him."

She could hardly wait to get home to try out the name for her pet. She ran to the barn and found the cat in the loft. She tiptoed over and whispered, "Mustard, Mustard, you awake?" The cat stretched out lazily and ignored her. So she dug deep into her apron pocket and pulled out a treat, part of a sugar cookie left over from her lunch. "I have something for you, Mustard, something good to eat." The cat sprang to life and jumped onto her lap. She squeezed him tightly, convinced that it was the right name. The next day, she thanked Josie for her help.

Mary always had more enthusiasm to get up on school days. She had lots of friends, liked the routines and did very well considering she started her education later than most. There was a definite pattern to everything that happened at school and Mary felt comfortable and secure.

Each day when the noon hour bell rang, the two girls would run and sit under their favourite apple tree by the riverbank, a piece removed from the others. Most of the children played ball, shinny, hoops, marbles or jacks once they had eaten their lunch. Josie and Mary were happy to sit and talk after they pooled their food. There never seemed to be enough to eat.

"I think that's all there is Josie," Mary said with a sigh. She lay down on her back with her hands behind her head. Josie continued to search through both their lunch pails for any forgotten food.

She sighed as well, "I think you're right, Mary. There's never quite enough, but what we had was delicious. I especially love Mama's baked beans even if I have to eat them cold. Usually there's none left after dinner but since John's been away, it makes a difference." John, one of Josie's older brothers, was living in a small town north of Innerkip and was rarely home. He was apprenticing with a wheelwright, learning to make wheels for carriages and farmer's wagons. It always made Mary sad to hear his name. After all, she had a "John" too. She missed him so much. Of all her brothers and sisters, he was her favourite. Mary longed to see his face, hold his hand and hear him laugh.

Mary stared through the apple tree branches, at the soft white fluffy clouds moving silently across the sky and then closed her eyes. She could see that photo clear as a bell, as though she was holding it in her hand that very moment. John was sitting on a barrel in front of the shed, holding Mary in his arms. Barney, their black shepherd collie was beside them. She remembered how John's big blue eyes, the same colour as her own, just stared at you, as if they might pop out of his head. He was only six, three years older than Mary, but really tall for his age. She recalled that he was always watching out for her, always protecting her.

"Did you hear what I said, Mary?" Josie asked.

"Of course, about John being away and all."

"Well, the important part of the story was the baked beans. Sometimes I don't know where you are," Josie admitted. Mary often daydreamed about her family but found it difficult to talk about them. Josie was polite enough not to ask; someday she'd tell her everything, but not today.

"There you go dreaming again. I know you're not listening to me. Wherever you are, it sure must be a nice place, cause you're always smiling," Josie added.

"Do you want to play hoops?" a voice from the distance interrupted. Laura was approaching the two girls. "I'll even let you look through my brand new kaleidoscope," she continued. She was friendly enough but Laura had so many clothes and toys that some days it made Mary envious. This was one of those days. Josie jumped up, eager to have an opportunity to play with a wooden hoop.

"You go ahead, Jos. I'm going to stay here under the tree." With that, Josie ran off to play.

For awhile Mary sat by herself but soon grew restless. She decided to take a walk over by the edge of the woods near the river hoping to find a few wild hickory nuts or acorns. The children often did this at lunchtime and then would have a contest to see who could flick a nut the farthest from the top of a thumbnail. She took Josie's lunch pail since the handle on it was much stronger than hers and would hold more nuts.

As she got closer to the margin of the growth of hickory trees, she thought she heard a rustle in the ground shrubbery. She stopped and listened...nothing but a little chickadee up ahead jumping around in the thicket and children's voices in the distance, so she continued walking. Suddenly she stopped; she was sure that voices could be heard, just ahead.

Mary got down on her hands and knees and moved cautiously in the ground cover. Then she saw them. She dropped down on her belly for fear of being seen. It was Billy Skillings' older brother Joe and Rachel Watkins. They were behind a big grove of oak trees, lying on the ground, clinging to each other.

The sounds seemed strange; Mary crept closer and listened. She had seen them holding hands behind the school one other time but this was different. They were actually kissing each other. Mary strained her neck to get a better view. Joe was very quiet and looked serious. Rachel looked sort of scared. In all of Mary's eight years, she'd never seen anything like this.

Mary was intrigued and very curious. Rachel was only twelve years old, and Joe only fourteen. She wondered what it would be like to be kissed by a boy. She wondered if she would have to wait four more years for it to happen. Accidentally, she leaned on the lunch pail, causing a slight rustling noise in the leaves.

"Joe, did you hear that?" Rachel panicked.

"It's your imagination Rachel. Come on," he replied, and continued to stroke her long dark hair.

This tranquil riverside scene is reminiscent of the view of the riverbank area that Mary would have seen not too distant from the school. *Courtesy the Pettit Collection.*[15]

Just then the school bell rang. Mary, frightened of being caught, cautiously backed out of her spot and ran back to where she and Josie had eaten their lunch. Much to her chagrin, she discovered that, in her haste, she had left Josie's lunch pail behind on the ground. Too late now. She gathered up her own things and ran into the schoolroom.

A few moments later Rachel and Joe appeared, each walking in through their own entrance. He was carrying the lunch pail. As he walked past Josie, he dropped it on her desk, leaned down and said angrily, "You little spy, I'll get you." A confused Josie looked up at him while Mary lowered her head and began printing on her slate.

Later, Mary confided in Josie and told her the whole story. Much to her surprise, Josie showed no sign of being mad. Indeed she was more interested in having Mary explain in detail all that she had seen and heard.

Yes, Mary truly enjoyed her first year of formal schooling. She developed friendships and began to accumulate special memories, albeit some more positive than others.

Mary would never forget the time that Josie found her in the woods several weeks after she had witnessed the incident with Rachel and Joe. She had gone back to the grove of oak trees where she spotted the young couple. Sensing something special about the small clearing beside the trees, she lay down on the ground in that same spot and wrapped her arms tightly around herself. As she closed her eyes, Mary imagined "his" arms around her. She did not know who the "he" was, but she did know he was very handsome and certainly did not have red hair or freckles. Even though her best friend had red hair, it was not her favourite colour. And he said the most wonderful things, things no-one had ever said to her. It felt so real, his head nuzzling the side of her neck as he whispered to her softly. Eyes closed, she rolled on the hard ground, hugging herself and moaning softly. Suddenly she heard screaming. It was Josie, standing above her head, yelling hysterically.

"Mary, what is it? Are you having a fit?"

Immediately, Mary realized that Josie thought she was having a seizure, similar to the ones Mrs. Jacques sometimes had. Instinctively she started to laugh. She continued to roll on the ground and giggle uncontrollably which even upset Josie more. Although a bit embarrassed, when Mary finally caught her breath she told Josie what she had been doing. Both girls sat on the ground holding their sides, doubling over with laughter. Mary made Josie promise not to tell anyone. As time went by, she and Josie became the very best of friends.

Some of Mary's fondest memories were of her times at school. Arbor Day in May was one of them. School books were cast aside, the children cleaned the school as well as the grounds. They planted a special tree in the yard and enjoyed a leisurely walk in the nearby woods.

Lockout Day[16] was another annual event. This was a day when the students arrived early, climbed in through a window to unlock the door (the smallest child had this job) and quite literally locked the teacher out. Finally, after some coaxing, the teacher was let in. Since everyone was guilty, no-one was punished. Usually, but of course this depended on the teacher, the rest of the day was declared a holiday. The children would go down to the river and take turns on the birch tree swing or play ball in the little clearing beside the schoolhouse.

"Smoking out the teacher" was another prank that the older boys played on Miss McGuire. They would climb onto the schoolhouse roof and cover the chimney with tree branches. In the winter when the stove was lit, the room would fill with smoke, the children had to get out and, of course, miss some "valuable" learning time. Students were severely punished for this as it was potentially very dangerous.

Another special event was the school picnic, the last day in June. Then, the pupils got to spend the whole day outdoors, taking part in races and games like tug-of-war across the river. Sometimes they would play shinny. Even the girls were allowed to participate because it was the end of the year. They used tree branches for sticks and if no-one had a proper leather ball, a crushed tin can or a ball of yarn would do.

But by far her favourite memory of "Willowcreek School," Mary's special name for Blandford School, was the Christmas concert when she was ten.

Eight

CHRISTMAS PAGEANT

"The job of adults to whom children were given was to shape their crude material into finished form and to do so through the application of work and discipline. This was not always a pleasant task. None of them are angels; all of them have human passions to be corrected, and often will give a good deal of trouble to those who undertook the task. The task of those who received such children was to take them and drill them into usefulness."[17]

December, 1894

EACH CHRISTMAS since Mary's arrival at the Jacques, she had received a letter from her older sister, Carolyn, who lived in Scotland. It had been with reluctance that Mr. Murray, the agency inspector, told Carolyn that Mary was living at the Jacques farm, near Innerkip. He preferred not to do so, but felt compelled by her compassionate letter. Mr. Murray also somewhat doubted that mail from Scotland would ever reach the farm. But fortunately for Mary, it had.

Mary looked forward to December for two reasons: one was the Christmas pageant and the other was the arrival of her sister's gift from

Scotland. This, as well as an orange and a sweet from the Jacques, were her only Christmas presents. Carolyn, who was now sixteen, always sent something handmade accompanied by a letter.

This year's parcel arrived at the post office in town mid-November but by the time it reached Mary, December was well underway.[18] After getting into bed, she opened it by the light the moon reflected in her window. Mary was so excited she could not even remember whether she had filled the water pail or woodbox for morning. Further more she did not care.

Quickly, she tore off the brown wrapping. Inside she found a pair of woollen mittens, cornflower blue, her favourite colour. Then she opened the letter:

Dear Mary,

I miss you so much. Each year as I write I try to imagine what you look like. You were so little when we had to say good-bye. I hope you are doing well on the farm. As you already know, I got married last year. I'm living in Glasgow, not far from Rutherglen where we all used to live. I now have a little boy, William, named after Pa and our brother Will. He's almost 6 months old and growing real fast.

Pa died last winter. He had a heart attack. Try not to be too sad, Mary, he was never the same after he lost Mama. I don't hear from our brothers or Emma. I hope they are alright. You are in my prayers every night.

Love, Carolyn

Carolyn's letter made her so homesick. Mary cried as she read it. Wiping away her tears, she read it again, carefully folded the letter in half and put it under her pillow. Later, she would tuck it away in the faded red tea caddy, where she had saved Carolyn's other two letters.

––––––––

Each year the school organized a Christmas pageant or an evening concert of some kind. Everyone in the community looked forward to the event since there were so few social outings that brought rural folks together. Parents loved to see their children show off their talents and it was understood by the teacher that every child should take part. The kind of concert varied according to the personality of the teacher in charge, but no matter how well-organized the concert was, someone would fall ill and not be there. Influenza and quinsy were common ailments as well as the dreaded disease infantile paralysis. Yet every year, healthy children or not, the concert would go on.

This was Miss McGuire's fifth year at the school. She felt strongly that each one of her students should participate in some way. For this year's pageant she had chosen "The Little Shepherd Boy." Music, dancing and acting told the story of how a poor farm boy, who tended sheep, managed to buy a gift for his mother at Christmas time. The shepherd boy played by one of the senior students, Absalom Taylor, had two sisters. Mary was given the part of one of the sisters. She was thrilled. In the past she had been in the choir, but then so was everyone else without a part. This year she had a "real" part with some speaking lines. It also meant that she would be on stage with Ab. He had the biggest brown eyes and had dimples when he smiled, which was often. Since September, Mary had been watching him, but Ab did not seem to notice her. Maybe he would now.

"What if Mary doesn't come to the pageant?" Jenny McLean asked. Mary knew Jenny wanted the part herself.

"Let's not worry about things that might never happen, Jenny," replied the teacher patiently, although the thought had occurred to her as well.

By early December, Mary had her lines memorized and was practising them in front of Mustard daily. She would say her line, wait an appropriate interval since she knew everyone else's part too, and then deliver her next line. Not always a good audience, Mustard sometimes fell asleep.

As the weather grew colder, Mrs. Jacques became more difficult to please. Her health continued to deteriorate and as a result, in her anger and fear, she would "peck away" at Mary. Mary had no-one to turn to for help. To get her chores done before leaving for school, she was up by four in the morning during the winter months. Mary worked hard and was often hungry because of a scanty breakfast. Her two mile walk to school, especially after the first snow, was tiring. Soon Mary began to look sickly.

Miss McGuire was becoming concerned. She could see the little girl did not look well. One morning, she asked Mary to stay behind after she dismissed the children for recess.

"Mary, are you feeling alright?" she asked.

"I'm very tired…sometimes I feel faint," Mary replied, hesitantly.

"How often do you have these fainting spells, Mary?"

"Oh, just once in awhile, Miss." Mary didn't want her to speak to Mrs. Jacques. The teacher suggested she stay in from recess and rest.

Mary began to arrive later and later for school. Aware that Mary was at a disadvantage, Miss McGuire overlooked her tardiness unless the other students deliberately made a fuss.

After school, Mary walked another two miles home, quickly changed her clothes, carried in the firewood and mixed buttermilk and bran for the dogs. She did this without even a piece of bread for a snack and supper would not be until six. By then she was almost too tired to eat. If she complained of not feeling well, Mrs. Jacques would not let her go to school. School was the only thing Mary loved; well, that and Josie and Mustard.

Two weeks before the pageant, Mary became very ill. She was "overcome with quinsy" so severely that the Jacques sent for the village doctor, Dr. Chesney, who happened to be Josie's uncle. As the local doctor, he was familiar with the entire neighbourhood and was not entirely unaware of Mary's home situation.

The white-haired, bearded doctor arrived by horse and cutter. A kindly man, he had been overworked and underpaid for all the twenty-two years he had been practising medicine. Often, people had him stay for a meal or sent him home with a bushel of apples or a plucked chicken in lieu of payment for his services.

This particular night even Mrs. Jacques was concerned. After all, it would not look good if the girl died "while under their care." Mary was so thin and weak that Dr. Chesney advised her to go to bed for a week.

"This girl is run down from overwork, hunger and fear."

"It's too much for her to be going to school every day, simply too many irons in the fire," Mrs. Jacques replied, choosing to ignore the doctor's reference to hunger and fear. "She probably caught a cold from the others. We'll be sure to keep her home for awhile."

"But I have to be at the Christmas pageant. I have an important part to play," Mary spoke in a thin, reedy voice directly to the doctor as if no-one else was present.

The one-room schoolhouse had eight grades together. The classes were organized into "books" according to which level of reader each child had advanced. For this photograph taken in the 1890s the children have obviously dressed in their best. *From* The Old Log School.[19]

"Well now, let's see. You've got better than two weeks to get feeling spry again. I don't think that will be a problem," Dr. Chesney replied and winked at Mary. "I expect if you rest till then, you could certainly go to the concert. Don't you think so too, May?" the doctor turned to Mrs. Jacques for a response.

"Oh, I suppose so," she conceded grudgingly.

"Well, I'll be getting along now. And I'll be real disappointed if I don't see you on that stage, young lady, come December...," he paused as he gestured with his index finger in a gentle way.

"December 16th," Mary added.

"Yes, December 16th." The doctor picked up his black bag, put his hat on, nodded and was gone.

A week and a half later, Mary had recovered sufficiently to return to school. On the first day back, she stayed behind at recess time. This was her usual practice if she wanted to speak to Miss McGuire privately.

"Did you want something, Mary?"

"I was wondering, Miss, if you gave my part to somebody else."

"Why would I do that, Mary?"

"I know I've missed some school but I know my part real well. I've been practising in front of Mustard." The last part she hadn't intended to say.

"Mustard?"

"Mustard's my cat. He's my best friend in the whole world."Then feeling a bit guilty, she added, "Except for Josie that is."

The teacher smiled at Mary's honesty and innocence. "Well, if you've been practising your lines, there is no reason you shouldn't have the part, is there, Mary?"

"No, Miss. Thank you." She started to leave but turned back again. Biting her bottom lip, she continued, "What would you have done if I'd been too sick to go to the concert?"

Miss McGuire thought for a brief second. She simply could not bring herself to tell the little girl that she had already considered replacing her. "We would just change the story a little and the shepherd boy would have one sister instead of two."

Mary pondered this response. Words could not describe her feelings for her teacher.

"Mary—," the teacher's voice gently nudged her thoughts back to the classroom. "Would you please ring the bell? Recess is over."

Mary ran out to the front entrance and pulled the rope with all her strength. This was a job usually done by one of the older boys or girls. Miss McGuire had a way of making Mary feel special. It was obvious that the teacher had a soft spot for the little girl who lived with the Jacques family.

———————

The night of December 16 was truly one to remember. Travelling with the whole family in the Jacques' bob sleigh pulled by a team of horses was quite a treat for Mary. Even Mrs. Jacques came although it was very difficult getting her through the snow and into the sleigh. The drifts of snow glistened in the moonlight and the icy crystals made a hard crunchy sound under the runners. The little stone schoolhouse looked so different at night under a blanket of freshly fallen snow. Mary was grateful for Dr. Chesney and felt he was responsible for her being there.

Josie Chesney was given the honour of ringing Miss McGuire's small desk bell to get everyone's attention. After the teacher welcomed all the parents and children, the pageant began. The Allensby twins, Jane and

Tommy played a piano duet from memory and Jeannie Whiteside recited a poem she had written herself, "A Christmas to Remember." Mary felt it was far too long and wished it had rhymed. Then it was time for the choir. Both Jaques boys sang in the choir even though neither of them wanted to; they were much happier helping with the scenery.

Mary was very nervous standing at the front of the room, waiting for her turn. To keep her mind occupied, she peeked around the side of the curtain and began to count the number of babies in the audience. There were seven and only two cried a lot.

The play went smoothly except for Benjamin Bickell who kept forgetting when to open and close the curtains. And that was because he had trouble reading and the teacher had to give him a nod when it was time. Mary was satisfied with her performance. She hadn't forgotten any of the lines she had learned by heart and hoped everyone had been able to hear her.

At the end of the concert, the teacher thanked her students for doing a fine job and thanked the parents for coming out. After the curtains had closed, Ab turned her way and whispered, "You made a fine little sister, Mary." He grinned and showed off those two dimples. Mary did not know what to say. She just stared up at him. In all the confusion, no-one even noticed. When Miss McGuire congratulated Mary on speaking so clearly, she almost did not hear her teacher.

Dr. Chesney made a point of speaking to Mary as they were leaving. "That was a mighty fine speech, young lady," as he nodded to Mr. and Mrs. Jacques, "mighty fine." He smiled and headed out.

On the way home, Mrs. Jacques spoke proudly to each of her sons but never said a thing to Mary. This time Mary did not mind as much, because her teacher had already praised her. And Mr. Jacques had whispered, "Well done, Mary," in her ear, as the family clambered back into the sleigh for the ride home.

As Mary put her tired blonde curls on her pillow, she knew that her dreams would be pleasant tonight. A thin slice of the yellow moon shone through her little window as all along the rural road leading to Innerkip, families peacefully blew out their candles and lamps, one by one, and went to bed.

Nine

MR. MURRAY'S VISIT

"Each child was, in theory at least, to be visited once
a year, by an inspector of the federal government, a
man who would inquire concerning their situation
and satisfy himself that they were obedient and that
they were being given enough food to eat and an
adequate place to sleep."[20]

April, 1895

THE SOMBRE grey sky looked down on the muddy brown fields that
were beginning to thaw. The murky swollen riverbed was a reminder that
the rainy season had begun. Mr. Jacques watched the sky each morning
at sunrise to see what colour it was. According to the almanac, if the sky
was red it meant plenty of rain was ahead. He also had noticed that Tiny,
one of Daniel's dogs, had been eating grass lately, another sure sign that
rain was on its way. In spite of a great abundance of rain, with wet spring
making it impossible to prepare the land for seeding, the country folk of
Innerkip were happy to have survived another winter.

Mary began to anticipate Mr. Murray's arrival. Seemingly, he always
came in the spring rainy season just around the time of a lightning storm.
She remembered last year he stayed several hours longer than usual, the
storm was so severe. He had put his horses and buggy in the barn, but

even this break from the frightening elements was not enough, the team was still skittish when he left.

Mary was still terrified of lightning, but if she had a choice, she preferred the storm to be during the day. At least she would not be alone in the loft. Storms in the daylight hours seemed much less ominous.

This year would be Mr. Murray's third visit. Once a year, an agency inspector was to travel across Ontario to visit each child he had placed. The problem was that there were too few inspectors to oversee such a large number of children and great distances to travel between towns; thus it meant that the visits were extremely brief. Mr. Murray always headed back to Stratford after his day's visit with Mary and others in the general vicinity. He was concerned that he arrive back while there was still some daylight.

Mary hoped she would have enough courage this time to inquire about the whereabouts of her sister and two brothers. This coming to "check on his ward" once a year as soon as spring "would open" was her only chance. As the trees would be leafing out a little more on a daily basis, it became increasingly difficult for Mrs. Jacques to have a clear view of the road, making it hard for her to spot the inspector before he reached their laneway.

As the time for the visit approached, she began to "work on" Mary so she would say the right things to Mr. Murray. "You'll be getting your visit soon enough. I hope you remember what we do for you. That's right, a roof over your head and plenty of food, not to mention being with a Christian family. Are you listening to me, Girl?"

"Yes, Ma'am." Mary continued to wash the Saturday morning dishes without ever looking up.

"I know you need reminding. Don't be forgetting the situation you were in."

"No, Ma'am."

"We could have taken someone else. Then where would you be now, being orphaned and all? Yes, you're a lucky one, you are." Mrs. Jacques concluded with a satisfied grin. Her personal convictions were often strengthened by her monologues.

Mary wished that Mrs. Jacques would call her by her name instead of referring to her as "a lucky one," "Girl" or "orphan," but she knew by the tone of Mrs. Jacques' voice that Mr. Murray was expected soon. Mary not only remembered him from previous visits, but also from her time at Stratford.

He was a tall, dark-haired man with gentle eyes and very white and clean hands. Mary knew that was because he never worked the fields. He had explained his job to her before she went to live with the Jacques.

"My job is to visit all the children we've placed. So I will see you once a year. It is important for me to know that you're all right, Mary" he said kindly. "Each time I visit, we will sit down together, just you and I, so you can tell me how you're doing. How does that sound, Mary?"

"Fine, Sir."

"If you have something you would like me to know, you must tell me then. But remember, most folks are country people and do not have a lot. As long as you are fed, clothed and living in a Christian way, you must be thankful. Do you understand what I am saying, Mary?"

The seven-year-old child nodded her head slowly and looked up at the tall man.

"I think so."

"Good. I am glad we have had this chat," he said with a smile.

"Mary, how long is it going to take you to finish those dishes? Fetch the water, Girl, and be quick about it," snapped Mrs. Jacques. As soon as she uttered those words, her facial expression changed abruptly. "Never mind the dishes, take off your apron and come sit at the table with me awhile," she said in a much more genial tone, and nervously patted the chair beside her. Mary knew her visitor had arrived and it was time to stop working.

She moved to the table and sat down. It felt strange. She was unaccustomed to sitting idly even though she had been in this house almost three years. In many ways Mary felt her time with the Jacques had been much longer. They sat silently and listened to the sound of the horses' hooves and the buggy coming down their lane.

Almost immediately after he had tethered the team, Mr. Murray knocked on the door. "Please come in," Mrs. Jacques responded, putting on her "best" face.

"Good morning, Mrs. Jacques, Mary," Mr. Murray said as he nodded, smiled and removed his black bowler hat.

Brief visits to "home children" were made annually, usually about the same time every year. Reports were to be completed on each child according to regulations. Many miles would be covered by horse and buggy. *Barry Hoskins, Heritage Cards*

"Please do sit down, Mr. Murray. Mary and I were just about to have morning tea. Would you care to join us?"

"No, thank you just the same. I have several stops today and many miles to travel, so I best not take the time. What I would like is to have a few words with Mary alone."

"Of course," Mrs. Jacques said, as if she welcomed this and knowing full well that this was the routine. "I'll go into the parlour and read for a bit." She wheeled herself out of the kitchen, smiling her best smile.

Mary had not moved the whole time. She doubted that Mrs. Jacques would be reading a book in the adjoining room. Mr. Murray sat down across from her, placing his hat on the table between them. He waited until he felt Mrs. Jacques had gone.

"Now, Mary, let us talk," he said, reaching into his breast pocket for his little notebook. "Stand up and let me have a look at you." His arm gestured upward as Mary pushed back the chair and got up. "My, but you've grown since I last saw you. How old are you now?"

Mary was sure he already knew from checking his notes, but this is how he started the conversation every year. "Almost eleven, Sir."

"Well, you certainly are growing up, Mary. You can sit down now," he smiled and waved his arm not unlike a conductor prompting his orchestra. "Do you have anything on your mind that you'd like to talk to me about?" he asked patiently.

This was the opportunity she had been waiting for—for some time now. "Yes, Sir, there is one thing," Mary spoke slowly. She could almost hear Mrs. Jacques pressing closer to the adjoining wall and listening intently, afraid of what the child might say.

"Do you know where my sister and two brothers are?" Mary asked timidly.

Mr. Murray appeared slightly surprised and uncomfortable with her question. He thought a moment before answering. He referred to his notes briefly and cleared his throat. While he had always hated to separate families, he also knew his job was to place children—most people only wanted one child not several.

"Emma was sent out west, Mary." He was always vague for fear children would try to find each other and disrupt placements that were working out. "I'm not really sure exactly where, but I think it was to a nice couple in Alberta who did not have any children. She was so young, I am sure she is nicely settled in her new family." Mr. Murray paused and cleared his throat again. "As for your brothers…well, the older one was sent north of here to a farm, but that was long before you arrived. He could have moved by now. The other one, let me see…I can't seem to recall much about that boy…" After a pause, he continued, "A farm too, I think."

"Will I ever see them again?" She looked up at his eyes as she asked the question, her own eyes brimming with tears.

"Sometimes it's best not to, Mary. They have a new life now and so do you."

Although he knew this was not the answer she was hoping for, Mr. Murray decided to continue with the interview, and abruptly changed the topic.

"I can see by looking that you are dressed properly. How about food? Are you getting enough to eat, Mary?"

"Yes, Sir," she replied.

"Do you have any complaints or things you would like to tell me?"

Mary dropped her eyes to her folded hands in her lap and then to the scar on her right arm.

It had been a cold winter's night that December, just a few days after the Christmas concert. The wind howled like wild dogs and the drafts through the clapboards made the house cold, damp and uncomfortable. More heat was needed.

"Where's that girl? Get some wood in the stove," Mrs. Jacques demanded from across the room. Mary never answered. She was sitting on her milk stool by the end of the stove with her head down. "What are you doing there, Girl?" Mrs. Jacques continued to prod. The oldest boy, Thomas, gave her a kick which toppled her off the stool causing her right arm to fall against the hot stove. At first no-one realized that Mary had fainted. With sudden realization, young Daniel screamed for help as he pulled her inert body away.

"Thomas, run and get the cream quickly," Mrs. Jacques ordered as she wheeled across the room toward Mary. All Mary could remember when she came to, was lying on the floor and Annie putting cream on her right arm which had blistered from the extreme heat. It was the only time she thought Mrs. Jacques looked frightened. She was a great believer in herbal remedies like poultices, tonics and hop tea, but even she began to panic when she saw the extent of the burn on Mary's arm. "Put lots of cream on her, Annie. We don't want her scarred."

Mary had no idea what had happened that night. She did not realize she had fainted from physical exhaustion or that Thomas had given her a kick because she was ignoring his mother. She did know that she had never seen Mrs. Jacques this concerned about her well-being. It made her think that perhaps the scar on her arm was not entirely her own fault.

"Well, Mary, do you have any complaints?" Mr. Murray repeated the question patiently. She hesitated and then spoke softly, "No, Sir, I don't."

Report on: Mary Janeway
  Address: c/o Daniel Jacques, Lot 4,
                     6th Concession, Township of Blandford
Date: April 2, 1895
Visited by: L. Murray
Health: Fair
Conduct: Good
Attendance at Church: Fair
Name of Minister: Rev. Ward
Attendance at Sunday School: Fair
No. of days attendance at Day School in the year: 65
Name of Teacher: Miss McGuire
Reading level: 4th Reader
Progress in Studies: Good
If receiving wages?   No
                     What amount? —
Amount expended in clothes during year: adequate
Any money saved?   No
Has the child good warm clothes for winter?   Yes
Sleeping accommodation,
has the child a room or a bed to itself?   Good/Yes
What sort of work does child do?   Chores in general
If a girl, can she sew?   Yes
Knit?   No
Has the child written to the Inspector this year?   No
General Remarks: This girl has a good Christian home.
Name of Inspector: L. Murray
Date: April 1895–April 1896[21]

To date Mary had lived most of her short life in fear: fear of authority and fear of reprisal. She knew better than to share her stories of ill-treatment, forced labour and deprivation. For if she did, these would only get worse. Mr. Murray may have believed that Mrs. Jacques was in the parlour reading, but Mary knew otherwise. Perhaps he did too.

Ten

A FAMILY REUNION

*"While some households were welcoming, too many
were cold and unsympathetic, denying to their
charges even proper food and shelter."*[22]

July, 1895

"LAND SAKES alive…I can't believe what my eyes are seeing," exclaimed
Mrs. Jacques as she parted the white lace curtains in the front room. "Why
if it isn't Reverend Ward comin' to call. Mary," she called loudly, "Mary,
go quickly and greet the Rector. And, for heavens sake, be on your best
behaviour."

Mary gladly put down the potato peeler and hurried to the door as she
dried her hands on her apron.

"Why, hello there Mary. How do you do? I am Reverend Ward, the
Rector at St. Paul's."

"Good afternoon, Sir, I mean Reverend," she replied nervously.

The Rector was a small-framed man, about five-and-a-half feet tall,
with a worn, but gentle face that sported a neatly trimmed beard and a
handlebar moustache. He smiled at Mary. "Not to worry, child. I cannot
remember ever being called Sir, but I don't mind a bit."

By this time Mrs. Jacques had wheeled into the kitchen with amazing
speed. She was a curious woman. "Why, Reverend Ward, what a splendid

surprise. Mary, be a dear and put some water to boil for tea. I'm sure the Rector would like a drink after such a long journey in from town."

"No thank you, May." It was unusual for the minister to be on a first-name basis with one of his parishioners, but since Mrs. Jacques' stroke seven years ago and her complications with seizures he had made frequent house calls, his duty to comfort the afflicted. After so many visits, he felt comfortable calling her by her first name. "I can't stay more than a minute. I'm passing through on my way home from Woodstock."

Reverend Ward had been attending a meeting organized for rectors of Anglican parishes in the vicinity.

"I had an interesting conversation with my good friend, Reverend Beattie, from St. James in Holbrook. I believe I may have some good news," he said turning his eyes toward Mary.

"Would you by chance have a brother named William?"

"Yes, Sir" Mary answered without a pause. "I have two brothers, Will and John." Her heart was racing as she spoke.

"How old is Will?"

"Well, I'll be eleven next month and Will is four years older than me. That would make him," she paused, thinking about using her fingers to count, but realized she didn't need to do that. "Fifteen…fifteen years old," she continued, quite proud of her arithmetic.

"Hmmm…that sounds about right. Yes, I am sure that is the boy on the Lounsbury farm in Holbrook. Reverend Beattie said they have had a new lad since last March when Mr. Lounsbury was laid up. His name is William and he thought his sister Mary might be living nearby. Funny how the Reverend just happened to mention it to me. I thought of the Jacques girl right away."

Mrs. Jacques wondered where this conversation was heading. Mary listened intently. Could it be that Will was so close and she did not know it? Did Mr. Murray know all along but for some reason did not want to tell her? She vowed never to ask him any more questions about her family.

Reverend Ward turned to Mrs. Jacques and continued, "I am heading up that way next Wednesday morning and would be more than pleased to take the girl with me, May. That is, if you can spare her for the day. It is quite a trip and we would not be back until dark."

Mrs. Jacques cleared her throat and thought about his request. She prided herself in being a devout Christian. It was important to her that the Rector see her as a charitable woman. She smiled, "I guess we could get along without her for a day." Then she added, "Now I don't want her to think this can happen all the time. After all, her place is here you know." She spoke as if Mary was not in the room.

"Would you like to see your brother, Mary?" Reverend Ward asked kindly. He leaned over towards Mary and continued, "It is a good four hour trip there and back, and if it rains—well, we'll get mighty wet!"

"Oh, yes," Mary interrupted. "Yes, Sir, I mean. I don't mind the travelling part at all, or the rain," she replied excitedly. "I'd love to see my brother!" she said breathlessly.

"Then, it is settled. I will be here Wednesday morning at eight sharp to pick you up, Mary." He smiled at both of them, smoothed out his handlebar mustache with his left hand, just like he did every Sunday morning after the sermon, and was on his way.

That evening as Mary combed Mrs. Jacques' hair, May shared her real thoughts with the rest of the family. She dropped her crocheting in her lap and cleared her throat. The boys continued to play checkers and basically ignored her, but Annie set her book down and Mr. Jacques glanced up from the *Farmer's Almanac* that he was trying to decipher.

"Utter foolishness, wandering across the country to find a brother and for what? Just to turn around and come back where she belongs. I think the Rector is getting sentimental in his old age," she exclaimed. Having said that, she picked up her lace doily and resumed her handwork. Mary continued to comb her hair in silence.

"Now, May, it's not hurting a thing and it was real nice of Reverend Ward to offer to take her. After all, he's goin' that way anyway and she'll be good company. What's the harm?" Mr. Jacques replied.

Mrs. Jacques was surprised that her husband said anything. Usually, he ignored her. But she needed to have the last word just the same. "It makes no sense to me, that's all," and began to crochet more rapidly. Mr. Jacques picked up his pipe and went out to the barn.

For the next few days, Mary worked extra hard. She was on tenter-
hooks, not wanting to give Mrs. Jacques any reason to change her mind
and forbid Mary from going. Over the past years she had desperately
missed her family, and had tried so hard not to think about them because
it made her sad. But the Reverend's visit had quickly brought her memories
into focus again. The thought of seeing one of her brothers was almost
more than she could handle. As she washed the supper dishes and cleaned
up the kitchen, she began to think about her family back in Scotland.

*They were having a tea party in the backyard, just Mary, Emma and
Beebee. Mama had prepared a little lunch for the occasion—bread broken
into bite size pieces—and for a special treat a bowl of freshly picked wild
raspberries.*

*Mary had laid an old frayed baby blanket on the grass and arranged her
tiny blue and white tea set, a service for four, carefully in a square.*

*"Have a cup of tea Emma, dear," she said politely to her year-old sister. The
baby was already grabbing a handful of berries, totally oblivious to Mary's
dialogue. Mama, tending to her vegetable garden, was watching her daughters with amusement from nearby.*

*"And, Beebee, I mustn't forget you," she turned to the rag doll. "Do have a
little tea, Miss," as she poured the imaginary drink. She'd watched Mama more
than enough times to know how to behave at a tea party. Unfortunately,
Emma was not co-operating. By this time, she had dumped her tea cup and
crawled away from the table on all fours.*

*"I'm sorry that Emma had to go home, Beebee. You and me can still have a
tea party," Mary replied, sipping from her cup in a ladylike fashion, almost
relieved that Emma had disappeared in the direction of the vegetable garden.*

*"Well, I could sure use a cup of tea," replied a voice from around the corner
of the house. It was her big brother Will who had just come in from the field.
A great deal of responsibility fell on his shoulders since their father was away
much of the time. Typical of most families, the eldest son was left in charge
even if he was only nine.*

*Mary looked up and smiled. Will's overalls were covered in dirt and his
hands were filthy.*

*"Surprise! Beebee, we have company," she said excitedly. Will laughed,
rinsed his hands off at the pump and plunked himself down at one of the*

empty spots. Mary carefully poured the imaginary tea and he drank the whole
thing with one loud "sip."

"Ah…that was so delicious. I needed that after a hard day at work," he said
emphatically. Mary placed several raspberries and a small piece of bread on
his plate. They were gone instantly. She thought he could have shown better
manners and taken a little more time to eat and was about to say so when the
sky suddenly turned grey and cloudy. The mood of the tea party was changed.
Will knew how frightened his sister was of storms. It was time to go inside.

"Thank you for the cup of tea," he said politely.

"You're very welcome. Beebee and I enjoyed your company," she said.

"I really must be going," Will replied. Mary got up quickly, packed up her
tea service, grabbed her doll and headed for the shelter of the house just as
the rain started to come down. Mama, holding Emma safely in her arms, was
waiting anxiously at the door.

Mary knocked over the broom and the noise made when it hit the wooden
floor instantly brought her back to the farm kitchen in the Jacques house.
She picked it up and finished sweeping under the table. Her nightly chores
were now complete which meant she could go upstairs to bed. She let
out a big sigh. Would Will look the same? How could he? He was only
eleven when she last saw him. Today he was fifteen. Would she recognize
him? Would he know her? What if the Reverend made a mistake? What if
it's the wrong boy and not Will at all? She climbed the stairs to the loft
with these thoughts weighing heavy in her mind…

———————————

On Wednesday morning, Reverend Ward arrived at ten minutes to eight.
Mary was sitting on the verandah stoop between Ben and Tiny, Daniel's
dogs. She had been watching anxiously for him since seven-thirty. All
through the night she had been too excited to sleep, and certainly did not
want to keep him waiting when he arrived.

Mary was wearing her best dress, a little blue and yellow print with a
bow that tied at the back. She had on a pair of brown shoes which Annie
had grown out of years before. While they did not exactly fit, at least her
toes were not being pinched anymore. Since shoes had to be handmade

and were very expensive, she often went barefoot on the farm whenever she could, to save on the wear and tear of her shoes. She had brushed her unruly golden curls in an attempt to smooth them out but was unsuccessful, so she hid them under a faded straw hat. In her satchel was a light lunch she had prepared for the journey.

In her excitement, Mary chattered for almost the entire two hour trip. The Rector was a good listener. Having attended to the needs of his parishioners for years, he had lots of practice. Besides, the ten-year-old's innocence and her way of looking at things were both refreshing and enjoyable. Too often he travelled alone and he liked the company.

"Sometimes I forget I even have a family. But every Christmas, Carolyn, my older sister sends me something from Scotland. She's seventeen and married now. She has a baby and in her last letter she told me she's having another one. Carolyn likes to knit. Last Christmas she sent me a pair of blue mittens and the year before a scarf with fringe on it. She knows blue is my most favourite colour in the whole world. What's your favourite colour?"

The man paused. For all his years, he could not recall ever being asked that question. "Well now, I don't really have one, Mary. I guess I like all colours."

She persisted, "What's your favourite thing?"

"I like all of God's gifts, Mary, but if I had to choose, I guess I'd have to say the trees. They provide so many good things for people."

"Well, it's easy then," she concluded matter of factly, "your favourite colour must be green." Mary flipped back to her family. "I haven't heard from Will or John since I was seven. Emma, that's my baby sister, was too little to remember but I wasn't. It made me sad when we had to say good-bye."

Mary looked wistfully down the road. "Are we almost there?" she asked, looking up at her travelling companion with her soft blue eyes. The Reverend hoped and prayed that Will was Mary's brother.

―――――――――

The Lounsbury farm was quite a bit bigger and more prosperous looking than the Jacques' place. A large German Shepherd leapt out of nowhere to greet them when the buggy came to a halt and, almost immediately, two older people came towards them. Mr. and Mrs. Lounsbury had grown children who no longer lived with them. Because of their age and declining health, they decided they needed a boy to help out on the farm. That was when they contacted Mr. Murray.

The Lounsburys were expecting Reverend Ward and the little girl, but they had not mentioned it to Will, wanting him to be surprised. Upon their arrival shortly after ten in the morning, Will was called in from the barn.

Quite a shy boy, Will was not used to being around a lot of people. He could not imagine why the Lounsburys would want him this time of the day. The tall, thin, fair-haired boy, wearing stained blue overalls, a faded plaid shirt and with his cap in hand, entered the kitchen cautiously.

Will was visibly shocked to discover his sister standing in front of him. "Mary, is that really you?" he asked. His face went pale as he dropped his cap and ran to hug her tightly. Immediately, he felt embarassed as he noticed the three adults observing their joy. Reverend Ward slipped out the kitchen door with a nod of his head and mouthed the words, "I'll be back later," having stayed long enough to make sure the children were in fact related before he set out to meet his friend, Reverend Beattie.

The Lounsburys, feeling awkward at having witnessed this emotional reunion, did not want to interfere in any way. "Why don't you show your sister around, Will, and I'll make something to eat for both of you," Mrs. Lounsbury suggested kindly and motioned toward the door.

Once outside, Will wrapped his strong arms around Mary and clung to her. The Lounsburys watched from the window. "They miss each other terribly, Walter. Seems a shame they can't be together," Mrs. Lounsbury said to her husband.

"Catharine, there's no way, simply no way we can have that little girl here with us. We're too old to be parents again. We've raised our family. Little Mary needs a family," he replied with compassion.

"You're right, dear," she responded sadly, and quietly turned away from the window.

For a minute neither Mary or Will spoke. "Mary, I can't believe it's really you. Is this a dream? Let me look at you," Will exclaimed, releasing his hold. He grabbed both of Mary's hands and took one step backward as if to soak up every detail and put to memory what he saw. Mary was so overwhelmed, she never said a word. She couldn't take her eyes off her brother.

Work on a farm before the turn of the century required much manual labour. July was haying time. Here a load of loose hay is ready to be stored in the hay mow of the barn as winter feed for the horses and cattle. *Barry Hoskins, Heritage Cards*

"I had no idea where you were. I'd about given up hope of ever seeing you or Emma or John again." Tears welled up in his blue-grey eyes, but he took a big breath and continued. "I hated that orphanage in London. When I ran away, I never even told John 'cause I figured he'd wanna come too. Leaving you and Emma alone just wouldn't have been right. But I wasn't on the street long before I got picked up. They decided to put me on a ship heading for Canada right away, for fear I'd run again. And they're right, I would have if I'd had the chance." He let go of one of her hands, turned and began to walk beside her.

"I've got a pretty good place to live here you know. The people are real nice country folk and I get lots to eat. I work hard and they pay me a small wage. Except for the lonely part, it ain't bad at all. How 'bout you, Mary?"

By this time they were nearing the barn, a safe distance from the house. Mary sat on a pile of hay and Will plunked himself on the ground in front of her.

"Well," she began slowly, and looked around before she went any further. "I hate where I'm living, Will," she whispered. "Oh, I know that we can't be together, you and me, and John and Emma." Her voice cracked and the tears silently rolled down her cheeks as she continued, "but I miss my family." She paused briefly, composed herself and went on. "The people that took me in, the Jacques, work me hard. That's because Mrs. Jacques is in a wheelchair and can't do much for herself. I'm up at four in the morning and sometimes I'm too tired to eat supper," she stopped. Will was looking up at her and his eyes seemed so sad. It made her feel sorry she'd said those things. After all, what could he do?

"It isn't all bad. Mr. Jacques is nice to me and Daniel, he's fourteen, sometimes he plays with me. And, oh I forgot to tell you, the best part. Mrs. Jacques lets me go to school. I love school. Do they let you go to school?

"Oh yeah, they said I could go. I tried it one day and didn't like it. I told them I didn't want to go back and that was okay with them. I work in the fields, I have my own horse to ride and we have three dogs. Jake was the one who greeted you. He's the friendliest."

"I have a pet named Mustard. I found this cat in the barn a couple of days after I moved here. We're real good friends."

"That's nice, Mary."

Mary remembered that Will loved animals and enjoyed being out-doors. But it bothered her that he wasn't going to school. How could he learn to read, write and cipher if he didn't go to school? Mary knew people who couldn't read and write, like Mr. Jacques. She felt sorry for them. "What about friends?" she asked.

"I go into town every Thursday morning for supplies, me and Mr. Lounsbury. Jimmy Tilson's pa owns the cheese factory. I always see him in town. The money that Mr. Lounsbury gives me isn't a lot, but I can do what I want with it. I saved for seven weeks and bought a real nice ball. Want to see it, Mary?" he asked and got to his feet. He grabbed both her hands and pulled her up.

"Sure."

Mary said exactly what he wanted to hear. He dropped her hands and raced toward the barn, Mary following close at his heels. Behind a broken buggy wheel he produced a red ball and an old leather baseball glove. "The glove don't belong to me but Mr. Lounsbury said as long as I'm here, it's mine."

"Who do you play ball with?"

"There's a couple of boys on the next farm over and we play as much as we can, after the chores are done."

"I still think you might like school, Will. That's where I met my best friend, Josie Chesney. She's a year younger than me." She paused, unsure if Will even knew her age. "That makes her ten, 'cause I'm going to be eleven next month. She has red hair and six brothers and sisters. I don't know what I'd do without Josie."

"That's real nice, Mary," he replied as he slapped the ball into his hand wearing the glove. "Course you're still young and need that sort of thing. Me, once I turn sixteen, I'll be on my own."

"What'll you do?"

"I can drive a team, work the fields, sow grain, mow hay, milk cows, feed pigs…" Don't worry, I'll get a job," he said confidently. "Maybe then we can be together, you know, like before." He said this with less assurance. "Do you ever think about how it was before?" he asked quietly as he dropped the baseball glove to the ground with a thud and leaned on the edge of a wagon.

"Oh, Will, I think about it alot. I miss Mama and Pa so much. I get a Christmas present from Carolyn every year. I guess she must have found out about me from Mr. Murray. She's a real good knitter. But I worry about Emma. Mr. Murray said she went to a nice family out west somewhere. But I didn't know anything about you or John until Reverend Ward came by last week. I was so excited by the news. I prayed he wasn't wrong about you being Will. I prayed so hard God must have heard me. But I need to see John too, just to make sure he's okay, like you, Will." Mary was glad she got it all out in the open.

"Bout a year after I came here I heard that John was sent way up north to a logging camp," Will answered. He put a piece of hay between his teeth and continued to talk. "Don't know the name of the place but it don't matter, 'cause if you're in a logging camp you move around a lot. Why, he probably ain't even there no more."

Mary had tears in her eyes. Will felt bad for her, knowing she had such a soft spot in her heart for John.

"He'll be okay, Mary. Heck, he's gotta be fourteen by now. I'm sure he's fine."

Mary and Will tried to catch up on four years of missing each other. For all that length of time, there had been no one else that either of them could truly talk to about their family. Some memories were happy, some not so happy. Together they talked and they played out in the sunshine.

Will was very patient with his little sister since she really had never played ball much. About two hours after Mary's arrival, they were called in for dinner. And a tasty meal it was. Mary felt envious of Will's new home and would have liked to live there too. The Lounsburys seemed so kind even if they were quite old.

The time went by quickly, the Rector returned and Mary had to say good-bye. But not before both brother and sister promised to see each other soon. Will asked Mary to write down the name of the family she was staying with, the town and closest crossroads where the Jacques farm was. Mary realized when he looked at it that he wasn't able to read the information, but of course someone else could read it for him. Will tucked the scrap of paper in his breast pocket. They hugged each other tightly, said good-bye and Will whispered in her ear, "I'll come for you, Mary, as soon as I can, don't worry."

Going down the bumpy lane, she turned back to wave a final shaky good-bye, crying softly as Will's silhouette grew smaller and smaller. Reverend Ward patted her lap kindly. "There, there. Perhaps he'll visit you next time." Mary was afraid that she would never see her brother again.

Whether it was excitement or exhaustion she wasn't sure, but on the ride back to Innerkip, she started to feel ill. Mary fainted right in the buggy just as Reverend Ward was about to help her out at the Jacques. The Rector, who was weary himself, was concerned about the little girl. He too had heard the rumours about how hard the Jacques worked her, and she was a "wee slip of a thing." He shook his head, but what could he do?

The Jacques reacted with a strange detachment. "No doubt the ride was too rough for her," was Mr. Jacques explanation as he came out to meet them. "Not to worry Reverend Ward, we'll take over from here. She just needs a good night's rest." After dutifully thanking the Rector, a fragile Mary was sent directly to bed.

The next morning she was still feeling sick and was unable to do her regular chores. "I told you it was a mistake, utter foolishness. Just look at you now!" Mrs. Jacques prattled on, "You'll have sops for dinner tonight."

There was no further discussion about it, but that evening Mary had sops, stale bread soaked in water, while the rest had pork and potatoes. Even when Mrs. Jacques was silent, she still had the last word.

Eleven

BACK TO SCHOOL

"The most worrying thing—the thing that haunted
the imagination of some of the London politicians—
was the welfare of the children themselves. For many
of the children life in Canada was not charmed, and
that for a few it was filled with brutalities of which
no one dared to speak."[23]

September, 1896

MARY WATCHED at the kitchen window as Daniel and his father
worked in the fields, harvesting the last of the grain. Summer and early
autumn were the busiest times of the year. Crops had to be harvested,
the grain cut, threshed and wheat taken to the gristmill. Corn had to be
cut down, the cobs separated from the stalks and made ready for livestock feeding for winter. There were apples to pick in the orchard, some
to be stored in barrels for the winter or sliced and dried and the rest
cooked for applesauce and apple butter. She was happy to see this for it
meant the long summer was over. This year it had been an extremely hot
one. Mr. Jacques had commented on this more than once.

"Sure as I'm standing here, these are the dog days of summer," he would
say as he wiped his brow with the back of his dirty hand while he pumped

Horse-drawn delivery wagons would be seen on the streets of villages and towns across Ontario. *Barry Hoskins, Heritage Cards*

water into a bucket. Then he would put the long-handled dipper to his lips and drink it all in one gulp. His wife, sitting in a wicker chair on the verandah, would usually reply with something antagonistic such as: "Well I'd rather have this than those long, terrible winters where weeks go by and you see nobody."

Mary had eagerly waited for September since it meant she could return to school. Over the summer, she had written several poems for Miss McGuire, her teacher, who not only recognized but appreciated Mary's talents in writing. School was her escape from her daily reality and she missed it terribly. It was the only place where she was included in the laughter and felt a sense of belonging. She constantly felt like an outcast at the Jacques home and turned to Mustard for love and affection, particularly in July and August.

Most of all she missed Josie. Mary had only seen her twice this summer since they lived quite a distance apart: once accidentally in town while Josie's mom was in the drug store buying some medicine from the doctor who also served the community with a small drug dispensary. Josie's fifteen-year-old brother, Jimmy, had been ill since June when school let out.

"Ma's real worried about Jimmy. She even bought Dr. Taylor's medical book on herbs and home remedies," Josie explained as she kicked the toe

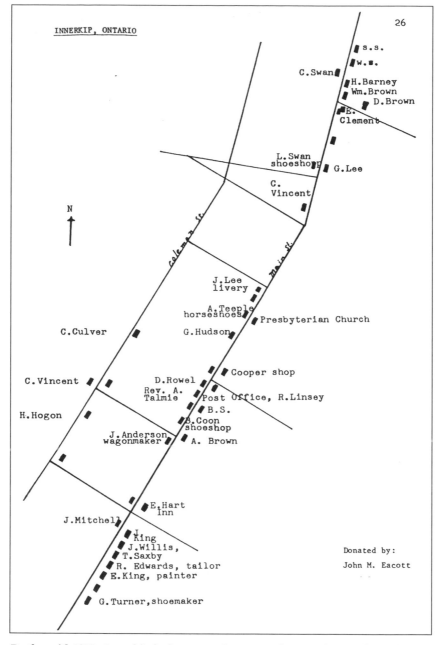

INNERKIP, ONTARIO

26

s.s.

w.s.

C.Swan

H.Barney

Wm.Brown

D.Brown

E. Clement

L.Swan shoeshop

G.Lee

C. Vincent

N

J.Lee livery

A.Teeple horseshoes

Presbyterian Church

C.Culver

G.Hudson

Cooper shop

C.Vincent

D.Rowel

Rev. A. Talmie

Post Office, R.Linsey

B.S.

H.Hogon

B.Coon shoeshop

J.Anderson wagonmaker

A. Brown

E.Hart Inn

J.Mitchell

J. King

J.Willis,

T.Saxby

R. Edwards, tailor

E.King, painter

G.Turner,shoemaker

Donated by:

John M. Eacott

By the mid-1850s, Innerkip had an extensive array of enterprises on the Main Street. *Taken from* The Early Days of Innerkip District.

of her worn shoe against the stony path. Dr. John Taylor, had been considered a quack doctor, a "Negro"[24] who called himself an "erber and rooter" and who lived in Innerkip. Many families kept his book on their shelves. Some folks thought he was just plain crazy, but Josie's mother was desperately trying anything that might improve her son's condition.

"Jimmy sleeps a lot and most days he doesn't work in the fields. He's still playing ball a little and as long as he does, I sure don't think he's that sick."

"Yeah, if it hadn't been for Jimmy, our team never would have won that game," Mary added as she reflected back on the baseball victory the last day of school.

"Mary, I didn't see you last week when the circus came to town," Josie asked, anxious to change the subject.

Mary's eyes dropped and she shook her head. "No, I was supposed to go...but I didn't," she added.

"There was this magician who swallowed a coin," Josie's voice became animated as she spoke, and then to confirm what she saw, she added, "For real, I saw it with my own eyes, and a monkey riding a donkey, a wild lion in a cage. They said he was really dangerous. And a laughing hyena." She stopped to catch her breath.

Mary's ears perked up. She had never been to a circus. The Jacques had planned on going and she was told she could go along. But Mrs. Jacques wasn't feeling well an hour before they left and, because she didn't want to be alone, Mary had to stay behind with her.

"Maybe next time the circus comes, I'll see it."

Josie's mother came out of the drug store and the Chesneys headed for home.

The other time she saw Josie was when Mrs. Jacques reluctantly allowed Mary to accept an invitation, which had been delivered by hand from the Chesneys one afternoon in early August. Actually, it was Mr. Jacques she had to thank because he was going in that direction with a load of wood and offered to give her a lift. Mary was thrilled with Josie's handwritten note which she had signed "Your very best friend." Josie had invited Mary to spend the night and had arranged for Joseph, her older brother, to take

Every village and town had a blacksmith whose role was critical to the well-being of both the villagers and the surrounding farm community. Here, a driving horse is being shod, possibly for the village doctor. *Courtesy Penhale Collection.*

Mary home on his way to the blacksmith's to get a horseshoe repaired the next day.

Mary remembered the visit with fondness. Mr. Jacques dropped her off shortly after noon. Josie had packed a picnic lunch in a big wicker basket with a red and white gingham tablecloth on the top. They went for a long walk in the bush behind their farm and ended up in a little clearing where they ate cheese sandwiches, pickles and juicy field tomatoes. Josie had packed a bottle of fresh cider and some oatmeal cookies her mother had baked for the occasion. Clusters of elderberries, picked by hand and then carefully cleaned, became dessert. Mary sighed as she remembered how good everything had tasted. She was convinced that food tastes better eaten outside.

Upon returning to the Chesney house, they played ball with three of Josie's brothers, Jimmy who was "the" ball player and the two younger boys, Mat and Jake. Mary felt so carefree, not worried about doing chores or being criticized by Mrs. Jacques. Today she had a taste of freedom.

When it was time for supper, Mary sat at the Chesneys' table with nine others. John was away working or there would have been eleven people altogether. Mary couldn't have been happier; she was truly a guest. Josie's two older sisters, Ruth and Sarah, had helped their mother prepare pork stew, boiled potatoes, corn and beans. Mary loved the dessert: cherry pie hot from the oven, made from cherries Mrs. Chesney had preserved that spring. Never had she tasted anything quite so delicious.

Probably the most exciting part of her visit was playing Hide-and-go-Seek in the barn after dinner with Josie and the two younger boys. By the time she climbed into bed with Josie, she was exhausted from running, playing and just simply having fun.

The next afternoon, seventeen-year-old Joe took her home. Mary hated to say good-bye to Josie and her family, there was so much love and laughter in their home. Why would she want to return to the drudgery of her own life?

Mrs. Jacques' sharp tongue nattering away about something abruptly put an end to Mary's daydreaming. Quickly, she finished the dishes and went off to bed before her mistress could find her another job.

That night Mary had trouble sleeping. Memories of the very first time she went to school flooded her mind. She had been so nervous then, but now it was different because she knew so many of the other children, and knew what was expected of her. She was dying to see Josie, Laura, Rebecca, Rachel and all her other friends, even Miss McGuire. As well, she was anxious to see Ab again but would not admit that to anyone but Josie. Mary was up at six, finished her chores in record time, and left the house by seven.

Chris, the Jacques' second eldest son had turned seventeen the previous April and was now working full-time at the cooper shop in town. There they made patented churns, cisterns, barrels, tubs and wooden buckets. Mr. Jacques, who was proud of all his children, always said "May, that boy is good with his hands. There'll be something for him using those hands, I just know." This meant that only Daniel and Mary would be

No country fence would seem complete without its chattering, inquisitive family of squirrels. *Illustration by C. W. Jeffries. From* Fences.[25]

returning to school, and since Daniel could hitch a ride with a neighbour he could leave later than Mary.

After saying good-bye to Mustard, she started out on the two mile walk by herself that crisp cool September morning, wearing her favourite blue pinafore. She was tempted to accept a ride from Mr. Milburn as he drove past with his wagon load of lumber, but having been caught on several occasions through neighbours who innocently mentioned it to Mrs. Jacques, Mary came to the conclusion it wasn't worth it. Besides, it was a beautiful morning and she rather liked being alone.

The birds seemed to be singing with more enthusiasm than usual. She stopped by the side of the road to see if she could find any ripe nuts. It was a little early for them, and besides, the squirrels were usually first. They seemed to know exactly when and where to look. She recalled a poem that Miss McGuire had taught them last fall. Mary had an excellent memory and was able to recite it word for word as she skipped along.

"The squirrel is the curliest thing
I think I ever saw;
He curls his back,
He curls his tail,
He curls each little paw,
He curls his little vest so white,
His little coat so grey—
He is the most curled-up wee soul
Out in the woods at play![26]

A small grey squirrel scampered down the road as if it were planning to follow her to school. As Mary continued on her way, she started to hum the tune "Mary had a little lamb," changing the lamb, of course, to squirrel. Her thoughts turned to her friends that she had missed all summer.

She remembered how Benjamin Bickell and Billy Skillings got caught stealing apples from the Allenby orchard next to the school. Mr. Allenby made Miss McGuire promise that the boys would be punished. She scolded them, but Ben and Billy told the others that she did not even look mad. In fact, according to Billy, "I think she was downright glad we did it. Mr. Allenby is an old grouch. Sometimes he lets the apples rot on the trees. He'd never miss the few we ate."

Then there was the time she and Josie went for a walk down by the river and caught six boys, one of them Daniel Jacques, peeing in the river. Mary was shocked, which made Josie giggle all the more as they hid behind a clump of bushes and watched. Once she was able to talk, she explained it to Mary in a breathy whisper.

"It's a game. Each one of them pees in the river. The one that has the biggest spout is the winner. It's called a spouting match. Boys do it all the time."

"Why?"

"I don't know why. They just do," Josie replied softly. Both girls were crouched down on all fours peering through the thicket. "Any more dumb questions?"

"Yeah, do boys always stand up to…you know?"

Josie's eyes crinkled up in her face as she tried to smother her laugh. "Oh brother, I think we've learned enough for one day, Mary," she whispered. "Class dismissed!" she said, imitating Miss McGuire's voice.

Mary began to walk a little faster, crunching leaves as she went. She thought about last year's Christmas pageant when Jeannie Whiteside, the angel, lost her halo right in the middle of the song she was singing. Everyone in the audience had laughed. Mary smiled. These memories reminded her of all the people and things that had been missing all summer.

Mary ran the final quarter mile past Milburn's farm, up the last rise in the road and around the bend until the little schoolhouse was in view.

Panting breathlessly, she stopped for a moment, feeling so exhilarated. She started running again until she was close enough to scan the schoolyard and spot Josie's red hair. Mary ran toward her, calling her name and, as she drew close, Josie turned and Mary fell into her outstretched arms. Miss McGuire watched from one of the windows and waited another moment before ringing the bell.

Mary found it difficult to be still and attentive during class. She looked around the room. So many familiar faces. Rachel had grown since June and Laura had brand new yellow ribbons in her hair. But she did not see him. Ab was not there. Her heart sank.

"Pssst...Mary. He didn't come back this year," Josie whispered as if she could read her mind. Mary mouthed the words, "Why not?"

"Had to stay on the farm and help his dad," Josie answered. Mary was so disappointed that she would not get to see Ab every day.

"Class, please pay attention. Summer holidays are over and our work for the new year must begin," Miss McGuire spoke firmly. The teacher sensed the restlessness in the room. She would compensate with slightly longer recesses but had to be careful for fear one of the older students might mention this at home. It was incredible how quickly news spread through a community. It was also incredible how quickly a teacher could be dismissed.

Rumours were circulating that Miss McGuire was being observed carefully this year because of some minor indiscretions, including being too compassionate toward her students and neglecting to enforce rules of conduct to the letter. The fact that the children loved her was also a hindrance to her popularity with the school trustees.

The first few weeks back were exciting for Mary. Having turned twelve in the summer, she was a senior now. Although a bit confused on the subject of growing up, she knew her body was changing and she was no longer a child. Most of the information she got was from Josie, who had older sisters and therefore knew a great deal more than Mary. Mrs. Jacques had simply told her that when it was her "time" to let Annie know and she would give her the necessary supplies.

At school Mary enjoyed the responsibility of looking out for the little ones and, for a twelve-year-old girl, she showed unusual empathy and ability to work with young children. Perhaps her care and concern for them was understandable in the light of her own background of deprivation and loneliness. Besides, Mary was extremely fond of Miss McGuire and was delighted that she had returned for another year.

She missed seeing Ab at school. She missed staring at his big, brown eyes and watching those dimples appear when he smiled. In her opinion he was the most handsome boy she had ever seen, the first boy she had had a special feeling for. She hoped they might run into each other, although it was unlikely since Mary was rarely included when the Jacques went into town. Despite this, she was as content as she could ever remember, but her best friend Josie was not. A different girl had returned to school that fall. Somewhere between June and September, the laughing carefree child in Josie had been lost. Mary tried to talk to her about this one morning recess while they sat under their favourite tree. Josie munched on an apple while Mary played cat's cradle, a game she had learned at the orphanage. All you needed was a piece of string and plenty of patience.

"Did you have a good summer, Jos?" Mary asked casually.

"Yeah, it was all right."

"You seem different to me somehow, you know what I mean?"

"Not really," Josie replied, taking a large chunk out of her apple.

"You're sort of sad even when you're happy," Mary tried to explain her feelings.

"That doesn't make sense, Mary."

"Well, it's just that you never really laugh anymore," Mary paused, holding both hands laced with string, motionless in mid-air and picked her words carefully, "like you used to."

"I'm getting older, that's all."

"I liked it better when you were younger."

Mary began to weave the string through her fingers again.

"Maybe you should play with Isabel Allenby. She's only nine. She laughs and giggles all the time," Josie replied bitterly, and took an even bigger chunk out of her apple.

That unexpected comment hurt Mary a great deal. She dropped the string into a little puddle, got up and headed towards a group of girls playing a quiet game of jacks by the school steps. In her heart she knew Josie did not mean it, but the tears still filled her eyes. The bell rang and school routines picked up where they had left off.

One afternoon later that fall, while Mary was walking home from school, she spotted a small horse-drawn wagon about a mile from the Jacques farm. As she got closer, she realized that it was her brother Will. Her heart began to race. She ran quickly toward his outstretched arms.

"Oh Will, you've finally come for me, haven't you?"

"Hold on a minute, Mary. One thing at a time," he replied. "I've got a job as an apprentice with a travelling pedlar. It'll only be for a short time until I get settled."

"What are you saying?" she asked.

"Just that I need a little time, Mary."

"Take me with you, please, Will," she begged, clinging to his arm. "I can help you."

"I can't do that. I'll be on the road for days. It's no life for a girl. Besides, you'd miss school, Mary. You know how much you like school," Will paused, gently freeing himself from her grip. He lowered his voice as though someone might be listening. "I have a plan. As soon as I get settled, I'll come back for you. And we'll find John, we will." He added, "I promise. In the meantime I want you to take this," he said and handed her a small white envelope.

"What's this, Will?" she asked.

"It's money, not a lot…it's part of what I earned at the Lounsburys. I want you to keep it, Mary. If for some reason you can't wait for me to come and get you, you'll need some money. Hide it in a safe place and don't tell anyone!"

"When will I see you again?"

"I'm not sure, but I'll be back."

Mary could see it was useless to argue with Will. His mind was made up. She tucked the envelope in her apron pocket, hugged him tightly and stepped back. "I must go, Will. She'll be expecting me and I don't want to make her angry." Mary started down the road, then ran back and hugged him again.

"Can I at least give you a lift home?" he asked.

She would have liked that, but decided it would be a mistake for Mrs. Jacques to see him. The less she knew about Mary's real family, the better.

She shook her head, her eyes welling up with tears. She took a big breath before speaking.

"I think it's best we say our good-byes right here. I'll be waiting; don't forget about me," she emphasized. Mary started down the road again. Tiny, the little hound belonging to Daniel Jacques, appeared from nowhere and walked beside her.

"That could never happen,"Will replied as he slapped the reins and headed down the rutted road in the opposite direction. He made up his mind after seeing her, that as soon as he could, he would be back to get her.

––––––––––

As the weather turned colder the walk to school seemed longer. The old black iron stove was stoked by the students more regularly. Mary could not help but notice Jimmy Chesney coughing a lot in school, but she was not the only one who noticed.

"Jimmy, I don't believe you're well enough to be here," Miss McGuire said kindly.

"I'm okay, Miss McGuire. It's just a cold in my chest," Jimmy responded quietly, but he continued to cough throughout the day.

Soon he began to miss school and even when he was there, Jimmy was languid and weak. Some lunch hours he would sit under a tree and watch the others play ball. Since he was a strong hitter, the team really missed him. That was when Mary recalled Josie's words "as long as he plays ball I don't think he's that sick."

The following day as the girls swapped sandwiches and shared Josie's drink, Mary decided it was time to talk about Josie's brother.

"How come Jimmy misses so much school? Isn't he afraid he'll fall behind?"

"It's not his fault," Josie replied defensively. "He reads a lot at home. You know he's real smart."

"What exactly's wrong with him?"

"I'm not supposed to say, Ma said so," whispered Josie as she leaned toward Mary.

"Why not?" Mary whispered back.

"Cause it's catchy."

"You mean you might have what he's got?"

"Maybe, but I don't think so. Ma's scared people will be afraid of Jimmy."

"I'm not afraid of Jimmy and I'll always be your friend," said Mary loyally.

Josie leaned even closer and whispered in her ear, "He's got consumption. Ma says the worst kind, galloping consumption."

"What's that?"

"I don't know except he's getting real skinny and hardly eats a thing."

"Is he going to die, Jos ?" Mary asked as gently as she could.

"Maybe," she answered softly.

Ever since last summer, when Mary had accidentally bumped into Josie, who was waiting for her mother outside the drug store, her friend had seemed different. Now, Mary understood. She wished she could do more for her friend. Mary reached over and picked up one of Josie's hands lying in her lap. She gripped it tightly. "I'll always be your friend even if Jimmy has gallo...whatever you said."

Josie tried to smile but still looked sad. "Promise not to tell anybody, Mary?"

"Cross my heart and hope to die," Mary spoke solemnly as she matched her words with gestures, "Stick a needle in my eye."

Josie was satisfied that her secret was safe so she quickly changed the subject. "I've got chocolate cake," she said proudly, holding up the treasured dessert. "First person to the river gets the icing." Having said that, she jumped up leaving her apple core and lunch pail behind and raced toward the riverbank.

Twelve

A DEATH IN THE COMMUNITY

"The suffering of orphan children in the early years
of this century, in Britain as well as Canada, was due
not just to poverty and neglect, but to the strong
conviction that punishment—beatings, whippings
and humiliations that broke the spirit of a child—had
a high moral justification. These punishments, though
not encouraged by the leaders of child immigration,
were commonplace in their time and carried out by
people who were acting, they were certain, in the
best interests of the children in their care."[27]

October, 1896

THE BRONZED leaves turned brittle and dry and in their own time fell to
the ground. Mary thought that autumn was the most beautiful season of all.
She could never understand why each fall the teacher's lessons centred
around things dying and returning to the earth. It had something to do with
lack of nourishment, but it didn't make sense. How could anything as beautiful as those crimson leaves be dying, when they looked so full of life.

Mary attended school as regularly as Mrs. Jacques would allow. It
worked out to be about three days a week. She was thankful things came
easily to her so even when she had to miss a few days she was able to catch

up. At the end of each day she always took her reader home, one Daniel no longer used, just in case she might not be returning the next day.

By a stroke of good luck, Mary managed to find a little job that paid money. For quite some time she had been polishing shoes in the Jacques household when Ben, the hired hand on the neighbouring farm, asked her one day if she would like to polish his boots for real money.

"I'll pay you a half cent for shinin' my boots," he announced. "How does that sound, Mary?

"Will you pay me each time?' she asked.

"Of course," he replied. "Whenever I'm over here helping with the ploughing, I'll bring my Sunday boots. By the time I'm ready to head home, if you've got them done, I'll pay you." She was thrilled but soon realized that polishing Ben's boots took much longer than a pair of shoes. Nevertheless, the money began to accumulate. After she'd saved for five weeks, there was enough to go shopping.

One day, instead of going to school, Mary hitched a ride into town, something else she was not supposed to do, and headed for Watkin's general store. It used to be the wagon shop until it had been destroyed by fire several years ago. As she entered the store, the air was fragrant with a wonderful blend of aromas from open barrels of molasses, fruit, cheese and exotic spices. Mary knew exactly what she wanted. Often a pot of coffee or tea was brewing on the big, black potbelly stove in the centre of the store to welcome weary travellers and encourage business.

"I'll have a bag of popcorn, please," she spoke with determination.

Since he didn't recognize Mary as a regular customer, Mr. Watkins replied kindly, "You know they cost two cents, dear."

"I have the money, Sir," she said as she untied the handkerchief she pulled from her apron pocket. She proudly produced five half-cent coins and after counting out four of them, carefully put the remaining one back into the hanky, tied it securely and dropped it into her pocket.

Mary ran all the way home, fearing she would be late getting her chores done and therefore have to divulge her whereabouts. Before she reached the house, she had finished eating the popcorn, having thrown the scrunched-up empty bag in the woods, and discovered the prize; every bag was to have a prize in it. This one was a little red tin whistle.

No questions were asked when she arrived home, even though she seemed a little breathless, until she hastily changed from her school clothes to her work clothes kept in the cupboard by the sink. As she took her pinafore off in order to put on her kitchen apron, the little tin whistle dropped from her dress pocket. It clanked as it hit the floor. Mary bent over quickly to retrieve the toy, hoping no-one would notice.

"What's that noise?" Mrs. Jacques demanded from her usual spot at the window.

"Nothing, Ma'am."

"Come here," said Annie, quite eager to take over for her mother. Reluctantly, Mary went over to her. Annie pulled Mary's arm and forced her to open her fist, revealing the little toy. Annie inspected it carefully, turning it over and over in her hands. "Well now, isn't this interesting! Where'd you get this?" Annie taunted her, then threw it to Chris. Mary turned to him; with that he tossed it to his brother. Daniel looked sheepish but went along with the game.

Mary looked right at Daniel. "I bought it. It's mine," she said.

"With what?" Annie snarled.

"Money I earned polishing Ben's boots."

"How'd you get into town?" Mrs. Jacques took up where Annie left off.

"I walked," Mary lied.

"You've no business goin' into town like that and spending money so foolishly," Mrs. Jacques continued.

"And you've no business making noise and upsetting my mother," Annie added. With that, she grabbed the trinket from Daniel. "We'll put an end to this," and promptly pocketed it.

Mary could not remember when she had been so angry and upset. For weeks she had worked to buy that toy and it belonged to her. "But it's mine! I earned it fair and square. You can't take it away," she cried. She made a lunge at Annie and grabbed her sleeve. Mary had never done anything like this before. Annie shoved her across the room.

"You've caused enough trouble for one day, Girl. It's time to peel potatoes and set the table," Mrs. Jacques snapped. Mary did not move. "Now!" Mrs. Jacques shouted.

"No! I won't do it. Do you hear me? I hate you!" she shouted looking straight at Mrs. Jacques. Then she turned to the others. "I hate all of you!" she screamed hysterically as she ran out of the kitchen and up the stairs to the loft. Mary lay down on her cot and cried herself to sleep. This was the first time she had ever defied Mrs. Jacques.

———————

Following an unusually quiet morning, and a very tense noonday meal, Mary was summoned into the parlour to talk to Mr. and Mrs. Jacques. Mrs. Jacques expressed her concern with Mary's defiant behaviour.

"No child living under my roof is going to fly off the handle like that. You best be reminded that we took you in when you had no-one that cared about you and nowhere to live. We've made a home for you here and we're doing the best we can. Remember where you came from," she said, pointing her index finger at Mary. "And you can certainly be sent back."

When Mary did not speak, Mrs. Jacques continued. "You are to take this pen and paper, go to your room and write a letter to Mr. Murray in Stratford." Handing Mary the stationary, she continued, "Tell him how happy you are here and what fine people we are for taking you into our Christian home." She paused. "And this evening when you do the mending, first things first…take the pocket off your dress so you won't be tempted again."

Mary looked over at Mr. Jacques who had not said a word. "It's best you do as you're told," he said quietly.

Mrs. Jacques ignored her husband's comment. "When you're done I want to read it," she went on, as if her husband were not there. "Until then stay in your room. And you best be asking God's forgiveness too. You can't live wrong and die right."

Mary left the parlour and climbed back upstairs to the loft. She wrote a simply beautiful letter full of lies just in time to come down for supper. She certainly did not miss having to prepare the food and also thought she might like to be a writer when she grew up. Actually, it wasn't such a horrible punishment after all.

———————

Things settled down in the Jacques household once again. Mrs. Jacques seemed to have renewed strength and energy once "the girl had been dealt with."

The following Sunday, Reverend Ward stopped to have a word with

The Church of England in Innerkip that the Jacques would have attended. *From* *The Early Days of Innerkip District* [28]

both the Jacques after the service. "I must tell you I was up in Holbrook last week. Reverend Beattie told me that the boy living with the Lounsbury family,—you remember Mary's brother,—well, the boy has moved out. Apparently he turned sixteen and thought he was ready to strike out on his own. So he took his wages and he went on his way."

"Did they say where he was headin'?" Mr. Jacques asked.

"No, they weren't sure, just that he was looking for work. He did say he'd keep in touch with Mary though. Nice to see him care about his sister."

"We'll be sure to pass the message on, Reverend," Mrs. Jacques replied.

When they arrived home from church Mary had finished setting the table and was scrubbing vegetables. Mrs. Jacques wheeled herself into the kitchen. "Spoke to the Rector today, and he said to tell you your brother isn't living in Holbrook anymore. He took a notion and he just up and left."

"Oh, really?" Mary tried to act surprised for Mrs. Jacques' benefit. "That was nice of the Reverend to pass along the message, Ma'am," she said politely and continued peeling carrots. Mary was so glad she had already talked to Will or the news would have been upsetting. In the back of her mind she was hoping that he would come back for her soon. If not, she would do just as he did at the age of sixteen—start out on her own.

The Jacques family tombstone in the Innerkip Cemetery. In the 1890s, the average life expectancy was thirty years. Many children died before they reached the age of five and the mortality rate was high in childbirth. *Photograph by Robert Hewson.*

By late November, Mary knew Josie's brother must be gravely ill for he had missed over a month of school. On the last Friday in November, Josie and her brothers and sisters were all absent. This was very strange. Mary was worried because her friend hardly ever missed school and usually told her ahead of time if she was going to be away. The day was long and tedious without Josie; even the teacher did not seem as interesting as usual.

Saturday morning as Mary went about her usual kitchen chores she heard church bells in the distance. She thought it was probably a wedding until she overheard something Mrs. Jacques said to her husband.

"Daniel, listen to the bells. They're comin' from St. James."

"I heard the Chesney boy has been real sick," he replied.

Mary listened intently when she heard them refer to Josie's family. There was a long pause in the front room while the bells tolled.

"Fifteen, Daniel. They rang fifteen times," she repeated sadly.[29] Mary was confused by this comment. With that she was called into the parlour and asked to draw all the window blinds.

"But it's so sunny, Ma'am."

"Just do as you're told," Mrs. Jacques snapped. As Mary approached the window in the parlour she saw a strange sight. A black horse-drawn wagon, carrying an enormous wooden box, was followed by a buggy and several men on horseback. It looked like the Chesneys' buggy. An odd sensation came over Mary as she drew the blinds down and blackened the room.

Nothing more was said until ten minutes later when she was instructed to open them again.

Once back at school Monday morning, Mary learned from the teacher that Jimmy Chesney had died of consumption the previous Friday. It had been a bad year for illnesses. Jimmy's death meant that consumption had claimed the lives of eighteen that winter, typhus having taken eleven more.

This explained Josie's absence from school and the scene from the parlour window. In order to get to the Innerkip Cemetery, the Chesney family had to pass the Jacques place.

On Monday of the following week, the Chesney children returned to school. Josie was strangely quiet, but once alone in Mary's company she wanted to talk about it.

"It was awful, Mary. I don't remember anything like this when Grandma Chesney died," she began as they headed for their apple tree in the school-yard. "We all stayed up on Thursday night cause Ma feared the worst. Jimmy coughed all through the night. By morning he'd stopped coughing," Josie paused to wipe a tear. "He just finally gave up and went to sleep. That's when Ma said he left us and went to heaven." She paused and looked directly into Mary's eyes. "Do you believe in heaven?' she asked.

Mary had never been asked that before. "I don't know Jos...Do you?"

"Yeah, Ma wouldn't lie and say Jimmy went there if there wasn't such a place."

"What happened after that ?"

"We pulled the shades and lit candles so it sorta looked like church. Ma stopped the kitchen clock and turned the pictures and mirror to face the wall. We didn't go to bed that night either."

Mary was bewildered as her friend explained this strange ritual she knew nothing about.

"Why?"

"Ma said it's out of respect for the dead, but I'm not quite sure what that means."

"So what did you do then?"

"Nothing. We weren't allowed to. We just sat around mostly and talked about Jimmy. He was lying in a wooden box in the parlour. Ma said it was a coffin. Mr. Langford, the carpenter, made it when he heard that Jimmy was real sick. Ma had Jimmy dressed in his Sunday suit. He never liked that suit. Mrs. McLean sent an apple pie over. Scotts brought us a pork stew so Ma didn't have to cook. But nobody was real hungry."

"What happened after you stayed up all night?"

"We put on our Sunday clothes and got in the buggy and followed Jimmy in the wagon. Mr. Langford drove the wagon. We followed him right past your place, through town down Main Street to the cemetery. Did you hear the church bells?" Mary nodded. "They rang fifteen times. Ma said that tells everyone how old the person was who died so they'd know who it was. Of course, everyone knows Mrs. Anderson is real sick, but they'd know it wasn't her. The bells would have rung a long time cause she's real old."

Mary still didn't say anything. She was trying to absorb all these things she'd never heard before. Josie continued:

"Reverend Straith said some nice things about Jimmy and they put him in the ground. That part made me sad. It's hard to think I'll never see him again." Josie's eyes were watery and her voice got a bit shaky. Mary put her arm around her. "I miss him already," she confided.

All Mary could think about was her own brother Will. He was just a year older than Jimmy. Josie would never see her brother again. Mary felt certain she'd see Will. For once, she felt more fortunate than someone else. Mary looked sympathetically at her best friend. "Your Ma and Pa and your brothers and sisters must be real sad," she said kindly and then added, "and me. I miss Jimmy too."

The girls sat against the big tree and for a while, neither spoke. Finally, Mary broke the silence. She turned and looked at Josie, held out her hands, palms extended and said, "Friends for life?"

"Friends for life," Josie said quietly and covered Mary's hands with her own. It was their own little ritual they had done so many times before.

Under their favourite little apple tree, in the schoolyard at Blandford School #3, two little girls shared their sorrow and strengthened their bond as friends. For Mary, it was her first experience with death.

Thirteen

THE COMMUNITY CELEBRATES

"There were, throughout the entire history of child
immigration and for years afterward, grave reservations
over the inspection system—whether it was done at all
and whether, when done, it was done thorough."[30]

July 1, 1897

"I WANT everyone to look their best when Mr. Hilderly gets here. Girl,
have you polished all the shoes? Annie, put that green velvet bow in your
hair and for heaven sakes go and find your brother!" Mrs. Jacques was
referring to her youngest son who was nowhere in sight and hated
dressing up.

The family photo day which she had been preoccupied with for weeks,
had finally arrived. There had not been a formal family photo taken since
Daniel was a baby, before her illness, and Mrs. Jacques felt it was time.
She had chosen today in conjunction with the celebration of Confedera-
tion, a day which was observed locally, especially this year for the thirti-
eth anniversary. It meant all her children would be home to join in the
fun. As usual, a village committee organized the events, beginning with
a parade in the morning to be followed by a community picnic with games
for all. This year's event would be even bigger.

Each member of the Jacques household, with the exception of Daniel, appeared wearing his or her Sunday best. The men wore starched shirts and neckties. Annie and Mrs. Jacques wore long skirts and high-necked white blouses. For the occasion, Mrs. Jacques wore a cameo pin at her throat. Both Thomas and Chris had scrubbed their faces and slicked their hair down. They knew from experience that the more they complied, the sooner this ordeal would be over.

The photographer arrived at nine sharp and set up his equipment. It was customary to go to the photographer's place of business, but due to Mrs. Jacques' illness, he had agreed to come to the house. The family moved outside on the grass near the lilac bushes at the front of the house. By this time Daniel had reluctantly joined them. Mary hung back not knowing what to do.

She was dressed in her best which was none too fancy. Her dress was a hand-me-down from Annie, but Mary was so slender that it looked two sizes too big. Annie's favourite colour was yellow, a colour which did nothing to enhance Mary's fair skin and sun-bleached curls. And yet she was grateful to have a Sunday dress at all, considering she rarely went to church. Her yellow chintz dress had white eyelet trim around the neck, which Mary adored. In spite of the fact that it was too long for her, she looked pretty. She had asked if she could shorten it, but Mrs. Jacques had said no; "Be grateful for the gift. Vanity is not becoming."

Once the family had been positioned around Mrs. Jacques' wheelchair, the photographer fussed with collars and ties, much to Mrs. Jacques' delight. Finally he turned to Mary and said "Well now, what about you, dear?"

Mrs. Jacques interjected. "Take the food basket out to the buggy," she snapped. "I don't think the sun will harm it for such a short time."

"Yes, Ma'am," Mary replied and turned to go in.

"Mary."

She turned back quickly, so unaccustomed to hearing Mrs. Jacques call her by name and feeling hopeful she might be included. "Yes, Ma'am."

"Get my grey shawl from the rocker too. I may need it if it should turn cool."

"Yes, Ma'am." Mary turned and went into the house. She couldn't help but overhear the conversation outside.

"What a beautiful day, what a lovely family. On the count of three everyone!"The photographer waited until the family was perfectly still so that the image he captured would be crisp and clear, albeit perhaps somewhat severe.

Mary walked slowly into the kitchen. She had not really expected to be included. After all, why should she? This really was not her family. She dismissed the exclusion from her mind and began to anticipate going to her first parade and big picnic. She'd had picnics with Josie at school, but that was different.

The boys were allowed to change after the photograph had been taken. Once Mr. Jacques, with assistance from Annie, helped his wife into the buggy, everyone else climbed in and they headed for town. It was a crowded buggy for a family of six, plus Mary. Often she was not invited for that very reason. While Mrs. Jacques expounded on the virtues of family life, Daniel leaned toward Mary and whispered in her ear, "You could have taken my place in that dumb old picture, for all I care." Mary smiled. He had always been her favourite.

As they neared the edge of Innerkip, the festive sounds of the drum and bugle band filled the air. They passed the sawmill, Edward's tailor shop and the harness shop owned by George Campbell and William Wilson as they made their way down Main Street. By the time they reached Anderson's wagon shop and the cooper shop was in sight, the parade had begun. Even though the sun was under cloud cover, the weather looked as if it was going to co-operate for the day. Colourful decorations, red, white and blue bunting and Union Jack flags adorned every storefront. Special displays of merchandise had been carefully arranged in shop windows and on front stoops for the occasion. The shoemaker displayed his lasts, the foot-shaped blocks of wood he had whittled by hand in different sizes, and the finished products of handmade shoes and boots. Mary was impressed by the milliner's array of hats, belts, feathers and shoes, described as being all the way from Europe. In front of the cooper's workshop, Mary saw a variety of wooden barrels, buckets, piggins and pails. The silversmith showcased engraved candlesticks, plates and spoons of gold, silver, iron and copper.

A great deal of time and trouble went into preparing for this annual event. Many hours had been spent decorating farm wagons and assembling outfits to be worn in the parade. The prizes for the prettiest, funniest and most unusual costumes were small, but winning was important.

As usual, a "red devil,"[31] which thrilled the children, led the procession. A man on stilts with bright orange hair walked along the side of the road, tossing licorice and saltwater taffy to the people lining the street. Two men disguised as a donkey made their way down the street to the delight of the children. Since this was Mary's first parade, everything was exciting. Her eyes grew like saucers as the brightly decorated horse-drawn wagons passed by, cheered on by the exuberant clapping and calls from the crowd. Quickly, Mary was caught up in the excitement and waved at the people—some of them her classmates—who were walking and riding in the parade.

And then she caught a glimpse of him across the street. Ab did not see her at first and Mary watched him through the gaps between people and wagons in the parade. She had lost count of the number of gaily festooned wagons, becoming more intently interested in what was beyond them, on the other side of the road. Finally, he noticed her, smiled and waved. Her heart pounded in her chest as she waved back.

As the last of the parade went down the street, she noticed a young girl, wearing a large brimmed straw hat, standing beside Ab. She took his arm and they walked down the street toward the community park. Mary's exhilaration from seeing him was as short-lived as the parade. Ab's girl was beautiful and she was wearing fancy clothes too. How could she think he would be interested in her? She was just a little farm girl, plain and ordinary.

While a bit hurt inside, Mary quickly made up her mind that nothing, absolutely nothing was going to spoil the day, not even Absalom Taylor. She had so few outings that she was going to have fun! She was dying to find Josie and hoping to spend some time with her family too.

The minute the parade was over, people seemed to appear out of nowhere, some pushing wooden baby carriages with large spoke wheels, some with small children in hand. Others carried baskets filled with goodies. The crowd was heading toward the park for the next event.

Soon the community picnic was underway. To everyone's delight, the sun broke out and the clouds disappeared. Families set up at the usual spot on Thomas Hart's flats by the river, across the tracks from the train station.

Picnics were a favourite pastime. Wooded areas and riverbanks were tranquil, peaceful settings where families could enjoy each other's company with little or no monetary expense. *Barry Hoskins, Heritage Cards.*

It was a favourite picnic ground with a permanent closed-in cupboard for storing food and picnic baskets that had been built by the town for the sole purpose of picnickers.[32]

Families found one another and grouped together, with much friendly banter between groups, creating an overall feeling of neighbourly sharing. The Jacques were not accustomed to such socializing, mainly due to Mrs. Jacques' difficulty in travelling, but this was a special occasion and everyone was joining in the fun. Finally, Mary spotted her red-headed friend down by the riverbank. Overcome with the general excitement in the air, she impulsively jumped to her feet.

"Can I eat with Josie, please, Ma'am?"

She asked even before being invited to join the Chesneys. She was that certain she was welcome.

"I guess that'll be all right. But don't be getting into trouble or eating so many sweets that you fall ill on us. We've had our share of fainting spells with you," Mrs. Jacques said, pointing her index finger while making reference to Mary's last buggy ride with the Rector.

Ignoring the bitter tone of the comment, Mary raced off to join her friend. Josie, along with several of her brothers and sisters were playing stick ball. Mary quickly joined in. She always felt a sense of belonging when she was with the Chesneys and was envious of Josie's warm, loving family.

They had a feast of crispy fried chicken, stuffed eggs, cornbread and potatoes—the quantity overwhelmed her. She could not remember when she had ever seen so much food. Mary went back for seconds, something she could never do at the Jacques. Watermelon, chocolate cake and ice-cream were served to everyone in the park by the ladies of the Innerkip churches. Mary was not accustomed to having cake except at birthdays, Christmas and once when she visited Josie.

After lunch she joined in a watermelon seed-spitting contest with Josie, her brothers and several cousins until Mrs. Chesney stepped in. "Children, I hardly think that's proper!" she exclaimed. They were not only trying to see who could spit them the farthest but also if they could hit each other.

"Perhaps you could aim them into a bucket instead," she said with a smile on her face. Mary could not help but think how differently Mrs. Jacques would have handled this situation. The children giggled and moved their game further down the river, completely ignoring their mother's suggestion. Matt Chesney could spit them clear across to the other side and was declared the winner.

The agenda for the afternoon events was hectic. Young boys chased a greasy pig, the prize being the pig. Races for girls and boys of all ages were run and a greased pole to climb was there for those adventurous enough to try. This was followed by a game of hardball. At one point, Mary grabbed Josie's arm. "Do you see what I see?" she exclaimed excitedly, looking off in one direction.

Miss McGuire, wearing a pretty straw hat with a cream ribbon, was walking with her arm linked to a gentleman's elbow. He was tall and slim with a well-trimmed dark brown beard. Mary had never seen her teacher with a man before.

"Yeah, that's Miss McGuire's beau. Ma told me," Josie whispered as she licked the peppermint stick she had won in the girls' relay race. "Sure is good-looking," she added between licks.

"How do you know he's her beau?" Mary asked innocently.

"Cause they're gettin' married. Mrs. Allenby said so. And Ma says Mrs. Allenby knows everybody's business."

Mary looked concerned. "Does that mean she won't be our teacher anymore?"

"I don't know. I never thought about that," Josie admitted.

Mary was quiet and pensive. She hoped her fears were unfounded. She simply could not imagine going to school in the fall and not seeing Miss McGuire.

A game of ball between fathers and sons distracted the girls for the moment. All the Chesney boys played. No-one said anything about missing Jimmy, but everyone felt it. By mid-afternoon everyone was getting tired and the activities were winding down. Mrs. Jacques sent Daniel to find Mary.

Mary hugged Josie good-bye and reluctantly walked away. Both girls waved to each other from a distance. Going back to the Jacques became almost painful and Mary dragged her feet in silent protest. Over the past years, Mary had debated about whether to tell Josie how unhappy she was living with the Jacques, but she knew there was nothing her friend could do about it. What would be the point? Mary dismissed the thought.

Just as she and Daniel were returning, the mother-daughter three-legged race was announced. Annie lamented how unfair that was and her mother tried to console her. For a brief moment, Mary felt sorry for them. Then she thought of all the times the two of them had treated her so badly and she no longer felt so charitable. There was not one family race that Mary could join in, and there never would be. She watched from the sidelines and silently hoped Josie and her Ma would win. They came in third place and Josie ran over and gave Mary half her prize, a molasses twist.

By four-thirty, the picnickers were tired and preparing to leave. Mary just remembered passing Trachsel's hotel and the harness shop before falling asleep during the ride home. She woke up when the horse stopped suddenly in front of its own barn. Mary made three trips in from the buggy, carrying the food basket, folding chairs, Mrs. Jacques' shawl and her special travelling blanket. She then made hot cocoa for the family before bedtime.

Mary was so tired she never knew how she got through her chores that night. Finally, she went outside to fill a bucket from the well pump. Setting it outside the barn door, she went in to find Mustard.

She found the cat in the loft lying on his favourite part of the hay mow. Lately he had been sleeping alot. She hoped the cat was not sick. As she scooped Mustard into her arms, she spoke softly, "I knew I'd find you here, Mustard. It was the most beautiful day. The parade was wonderful and so was the picnic." She thought it would be best not to mention Ab or Miss McGuire since they were not the highlights of the day. She stroked the cat's coat as she continued, "Sure wish you could've been there too." The contented purring continued as Mary rhythmically stroked its back and sides. "There were so many things to see and do and wonderful treats to eat. Look! I brought you something." She reached in her pocket and brought out what was left of her half of the molasses stick.

Mustard licked it and Mary smiled. "How could I possibly forget you?" she said, squeezing the cat even more tightly.

"Where are you, Girl?" Annie's sharp voice, coming from the side door pierced the quiet of the night like an unwelcome intruder. "Who're you talking to?" she demanded.

Mary set the cat down gently in the hay, kissed the top of its head and climbed down the loft quickly. Mustard continued to lick the candy. As she ran to the house, she grabbed the pail of water. "No-body," she answered, "Just getting water for tomorrow, that's all." Turning back toward the barn where Mustard lay safely undiscovered, she whispered, "Good night."

Fourteen

PROBLEMS AT THE GRISTMILL

"Notwithstanding all the complaints that have been
made against child immigration, it is only reasonable
to suppose that if the work were suddenly stopped
many a farm home would be in a quandry to know
how to get along."[33]

August, 1897

IT HAD been a hot, humid morning and Thomas was grateful he could
sit under the shade of a tree and eat the lunch which Mary had packed for
him. Mary wished she could have gone with Thomas and spent a day at
the mill but knew that there was no point in asking Mrs. Jacques for
permission. Thank heavens this was not a busy day or lunchtime would
have been forgotten. As he finished his cheese sandwich, he pondered. In
his own quiet way Thomas was content with his job at the mill. He had
learned a lot from Charles Press and he felt optimistic about his future.
As he bit into an apple, he remembered his first day on the mill site. He
was just a boy then. Charles Press had walked him around the property
explaining how the gristmill worked.

"Thomas, this wheel is the most powerful piece of machinery but without
water to turn it—it's nothing," he said, pointing to the large waterwheel

This well-preserved mill is now an historical museum. The three-storey stone building provides an impression of the structure of early mills, such as the one described for Innerkip. *From* The Pioneer Farmer and Backwoodsman.[34]

with paddles around its outside rim. Silent and motionless, it did not look very powerful to the young lad, but he said nothing.

They went around the corner to view a quiet pond, the millpond and beyond it, the mill dam. "From this here millpond, water is carried to the mill through a channel called a millrace," Charles explained, pointing as he went. "It's directed to the top of the wheel through a trough. See, it's over there. That's called the sluiceway. When the sluicegate is open, the water spills into those rims on the outside of the wheel—buckets are what some folks call them. And that's what turns it." Thomas was a bit confused by all this information but pretended to understand.

Charles smiled, turned and opened the sluicegate. Seeing is believing. Thomas' eyes widened as he watched the water roll down the trough and splash onto the first wheel rim. The wheel began to turn, slowly and steadily. And the whole mill began to shake and groan.

"Let's go inside and see what's happening," the miller said. The stone building looked like a tall barn. The first floor held the gears, the second floor was where the grinding took place and the third was used strictly as a storage place for both grain and flour. Charles patiently explained everything. It was far too much to absorb in one day, but Thomas was duly impressed.

By now he had finished his lunch, and leaning back against the tree, he closed his eyes. While Thomas was not someone who lived in the past, he enjoyed reflecting on it from time to time. He realized he had learned so much since then about the mill, the miller, his wife Martha and the villagers in town. He liked people and he liked his job.

"Wake up, Thomas," Charles said as he shook him gently. "This is a lunch break, not a day off." Thomas rubbed his eyes and realized he had almost dozed off. Leaping to his feet, he ran to serve a customer he hoped had not been waiting long.

Next month would mark his fifth anniversary. For the most part he found Charles Press a reasonable man to work for, demanding but fair. For his part, Thomas was not lazy, and certainly not afraid of hard work.

An apprenticeship usually lasted anywhere from four to seven years and Thomas had put in his time. He had swept floors, unloaded wagons and fed the mill cats until Mr. Press decided he was ready to take on more responsibility. Usually the miller's children would have done those chores, but Thomas was glad that Charles and Martha had no children, or so he thought.

Charles Press had a fine reputation as the miller for the town. He could operate, adjust and repair the millwheel, gears and millstones. He knew how to grind different types of grains, from wheat, rye and oats to corn, without spoiling the flour. He knew his machinery so well that he could tell what was wrong by listening to the sound it made and checking the texture of the flour. A man that worked long hours without complaining, Charles Press was a religious man and was respected by the other tradesmen in town. He was friendly and brought customers up to date on village news. And very importantly, he was good with numbers and kept careful accounts.

Frequently, his customers could not afford to pay him money for his services, so he would take part of the flour he ground as payment. When he first bought the mill, he owned and operated the bakery in town, but as business at the mill flourished he sold the bakery. After that, any flour he took in lieu of money, he would sell or trade for food, other goods or, in some cases, land.

Before long, Charles became the richest man in the community. Along with wealth came admiration. Often the town miller would be elected to political office, but in his case he had declined. He told the townspeople that if he took office his mill would be neglected. That was partially true, but the real reason was his health. For a young man of thirty-eight, he was not particularly well—good health being the one attribute he was lacking. It was essential for the miller to be in top physical condition as he had to carry heavy bags of grain and flour. The job required much manual labour with everything having to be weighed on the grain scale table and moved to various locations throughout the processing of the flour. This is where Thomas Jacques came in. While he was a fine-boned boy, he was wiry and strong, capable of lifting what Charles could not. Soon he became dependent on Thomas.

Charles invited him to stay one night during a bad rainstorm and a pattern was formed. When the weather was inclement and travelling home late at night was impractical, it was just assumed that Thomas would stay overnight. Since there was plenty of room in the miller's large home beside the gristmill, it became an arrangement that suited Charles and Martha, a childless couple. Thomas did not mind the extra attention, and it was one less mouth for the Jacques to feed. But Mary missed Thomas when he did not return in the evening. As it was Mrs. Jacques' preference to have her son at home, she often was harder on Mary on such occasions.

Martha Press was a capable, kind woman who would lend a hand and serve customers when things became hectic at the mill. If Charles and Thomas had to work during the supper hour, she would bring them dinner on a tray. Their busiest season was late fall once the harvest was off and in the winter months when outdoor work was reduced. A few families still ground their flour at home themselves, using a primitive handmill which made small amounts of coarse flour. But there was no comparison between flour ground by hand and "stone-ground" flour from the mill. From the time that Thomas was first working at the mill, the Jacques took their grain there to be ground. They felt a certain loyalty to Charles since he had given their son a much needed job.

———————

It was past six o'clock in the evening of August 23, 1897. All the customers had gone. Mr. Weathersby was the last one to leave and, as usual, the most difficult to please. Thomas had tried to learn to like him, but his abrasive personality made this difficult. He spoke loudly out of one side of his mouth, a cigar constantly clamped between his teeth. Always he would claim that it was unlit as smoking was absolutely forbidden inside the mill.

Rubbing his tired eyes on his soiled shirt, Thomas proceeded to clean the millstones in readiness for the next day. He was so exhausted that, when he was finished, he sat outside on the stoop and stroked one of the mill cats. There were about a dozen of them who helped kill the rats and mice in the mill, essential to have for pest control. Fortunately, the cats were easy to please: you feed them…they stick around.

Thomas was just about to leave for his long journey home when Martha came over with a cold drink for each of them.

"Would you like to stay the night, Thomas?" she asked.

"Oh, that would be nice, Ma'am. I'm real tired tonight," Thomas agreed without hesitation. If he were not home by dusk, his family knew he was staying in town. Martha was an excellent cook and besides, it was no secret that he was a bit sweet on Jenny Watkins, Rachel's older sister who worked at her father's general store. Rachel, a year younger than Chris Jacques, was still going to school. Occasionally, Daniel would mention her name at the dinner table and Mary would always smile, remembering the time she had caught Rachel in the woods with Joe Skillings. Thomas was not the least bit interested in conversations dealing with the Watkins girl, unless Jenny was part of the story too. Whenever possible in the evening, Thomas would take a stroll through town, hoping to bump into her.

"Thanks," he added with a smile.

Martha could tell by looking at Charles that her husband was unusually tired and having Thomas stay the night meant that he would not have to start his day quite so early tomorrow. Contented with the arrangement, all three headed for the house.

"Wash up, Son. Dinner is ready and Charles will do well to stay awake long enough to eat," Martha replied with a motherly smile. In spite of her shyness, she was fond of Thomas and often referred to him as "Son" when no-one else was around. They ate dinner in almost total silence, Martha realizing that both of them were exhausted. Shortly after they had eaten, the couple retired to bed. Of course, Charles had indulged in his usual smoke on the porch before bedtime and Thomas had gone for a brisk walk, no doubt in the direction of Coleman Street where the Watkins lived. He too was home and asleep before ten o'clock.

It must have been around midnight or one in the morning that Thomas was awakened by a strange "wooshing" sound. There was an unusual light at his window. He leapt out of bed to see. Even in the hottest mid-day sun he had never seen such brightness. *The mill was on fire!*

Racing from his room, Thomas pounded on the miller's door, frantically screaming for his help. Charles and his wife roused quickly and ran outside in their night clothes to see the east corner of their mill aflame. Thomas was nowhere to be seen.

"Oh, dear God, have mercy on us! " Martha shrieked, her hands partially covering her distraught face.

"Buckets, Martha! Get buckets and ring the bell," Charles yelled as he ran toward the millpond. His wife seemed to be in a trance. She stood motionless. "Now!" He turned back and yelled. Instantly she pivoted and raced to grasp the bell rope. The incessant sound of the bell alerted all the neighbours; the repeated clanging, as everyone knew, signalled trouble. Throwing on enough clothes to be presentable, the men came running.

By the time Charles got there, Thomas, wearing only trousers and suspenders, was knee-deep in the millpond frantically filling two pails found in a nearby shed. He had not even heard the clamour of the bell, but within a few minutes the neighbours were there, hard at work.

In times of emergency, the townspeople of Innerkip always banded together. The most recent occasion was last fall when Odie's barn caught on fire and when the Shepherds needed money to send their boy to London for a special operation. So when Martha Press tolled the bell, nineteen men, ranging in age from seven to fifty-three, rose immediately from their beds to help. Working in unison, they formed a human chain, a bucket brigade. The "wet line" filled buckets from the millpond and passed them along until they reached their destination in an attempt to douse the flames. The empty buckets were handed to the "dry line" and eventually made their way back to the pond. Others soaked empty flour sack bags in water and tried to smother the fire. At first their efforts seemed futile,

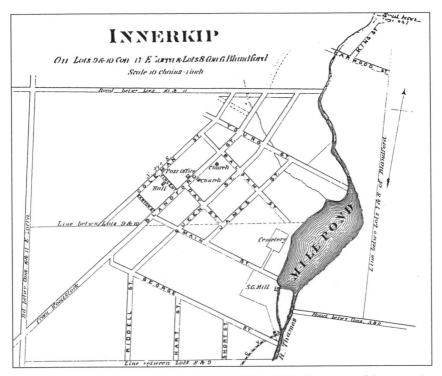

By the 1890s, Innerkip would have been a well established centre as this map illustrates. Note the location of the mill and the millpond. *From* **The Early Days of Innerkip District.**

but their dogged determination and persistence paid off. After several hours the fire was finally under control.

With the heavy dousing of the last of the flames, all that remained of the east corner of the mill was a bed of hot embers emitting a tremendous heat. For hours these smouldered, a reminder of the destruction that had just taken place.

Martha sat on the stoop at the mill door with her head in her hands and wept openly. Charles comforted her. Thomas and a few others who were still there left them to grieve in privacy. They went down to the millpond, sat at the edge and reflected on the accident.

"What do you figure happened, Matthew?" asked James Skillings, the local shoemaker. While no expert, Matthew always had an opinion he loved to share. Referred to as the joiner, another name for cabinetmaker, by the villagers, he made furniture, repaired musical instruments and built coffins.

"I think the gears were in need of oilin.' They just up and dried out and sparked," Matt said with authority, scratching his chin and watching Thomas for a reaction.

"That's impossible! I cleaned them myself last night and oiled everything,"Thomas said. He knew that this would be the topic of conversation at Watkins' general store for a long time. Opinions would be aired, conclusions arrived at and no doubt his name would be part of the gossip. For Thomas, the biggest fear was that he might be blamed for the accident. He had to find out what caused the blaze. Walking around to the far side of the building, he sat on an old stump; he needed to be alone to think. Sickened by what had happened, he wondered if, indirectly, he just might have been responsible in some way.

The few neighbours who had stayed dwindled off and the last of them left as the sun began to rise on the horizon. Thomas went to find the miller. Charles and Martha were still sitting at the doorway. They were relieved that the whole mill had not been destroyed and that their home had been spared as well. Martha wiped her brow with her blackened apron, leaving a smudge on her forehead. Charles tenderly put his arm around his wife again. Thomas stood nearby surveying the couple and the smoky remains. They were unaware of his presence.

"Dear, we must be thankful that the good Lord saw fit to watch over us. This time no-one was hurt and we can rebuild what was destroyed come spring. We'll manage—we always do," he said as much to himself as to his wife. Thomas wondered what he meant by "this time."

He approached them and spoke to Charles for the first time since pounding on his bedroom door a few hours earlier. "I oiled all the gears and millstones, Sir, just like always."

Charles turned and smiled, "I ain't blamin you, Son. It was an act of God. Nobody questions God."

"Still and all, I need you to know that,"Thomas paused and stammered. "that…that's all, Sir."

"Go home, Thomas. Take a day's rest. Your family needs to know you're safe, thanks be to God."

Thomas managed to hitch a ride part way home but was greatly fatigued by the time he arrived. As yet, his family had not heard about the fire but were thankful that Thomas was safe. Mrs. Jacques had plenty of questions, all of which he tried to answer.

"Let the boy be now, May. He's had enough," Mr. Jacques said after a bit.

As Thomas climbed the stairs to go to bed, he turned back and said to his father, "Was there another fire at the mill, Pa?"

"Not that I know of, Son," replied his father.

"Why would you ask such a thing?" Mrs. Jacques interrupted.

"No reason, Ma," said Thomas and quietly continued up the stairs. His mother knew there was more to that story and she would not rest until she found out. Annie would help.

––––––––––––

Several days later, Charles and Thomas sifted through the debris, looking for clues as to what had started the fire. Charles admitted that the millstones had needed his attention some time ago. It was unlikely that they touched each other causing the sparks, but he could not come up with any other suitable explanation. He concluded that no man, including himself, was infallible. His strong Christian faith helped him accept his limitations, but Thomas was having trouble coming to terms with it.

"I should have noticed when I did the oiling, Sir," Thomas said innocently.

"No, Son, a good miller leaves nothing to chance. I should have checked them from time to time," Charles replied solemnly.

"I'm glad I was here to help, Sir."

"If you hadn't stayed over and awakened us, we could have lost the whole mill, maybe our lives. Don't be looking behind, Son. Look ahead. You're a fine apprentice and I'm proud of you," Charles said as he put his arm around the boy. Words like this always made Thomas feel special. His affection for the miller, which had grown steadily in the five years they had known each other, had never been greater. His own father rarely showed this much feeling outwardly, although Thomas knew that his quiet father cared a great deal about him.

––––––––––––

That evening as Thomas was cleaning up before going home, he began thinking about the night of the fire when he had closed the mill. He had waited patiently for Mr. Weathersby, grouchy old Weathersby and his stinky cigar, to go home.

"Cigar," he said aloud. "I don't remember him having it when he left. Is it possible that he started the fire?" Excitedly, he ran to find Charles to tell him about his discovery. He found him on the first floor, in the midst of grey and blackened residue, counting bags of flour. His glasses had slid down on his nose and he was deep in thought.

"Sir, I think I know how the fire got started." Thomas stopped to catch his breath before he continued, "I think it was Mr. Weathersby's cigar."

"Do you know for certain, Thomas?" Charles asked, his facial expression changing dramatically as he spoke those words.

"No, Sir," Thomas replied disappointedly.

"Sometimes it takes a boy to remember and a man to forget," the miller replied. It was never discussed again.

Fifteen

ANNIE'S WEDDING

"Still, for hundreds and hundreds of the children,
the great misfortune that would mark all their lives
occurred not in the homes in Britain but in Canada,
where, through some fate over which they had no
control, they were placed with harsh and cruel
masters and endured not just loneliness and deprivation but forms of brutality that went far beyond
the ordinary punishments of the day."[35]

September–December, 1897

IT TOOK Annie only a little over a week to find out what her mother
wanted to know. Thomas' seemingly innocent question about the possibil-
ity of a previous fire at the mill would not allow his mother a restful night
until she got to the bottom of the mystery.

Annie went right to Mrs. Allenby, the town gossip who lived near the
schoolhouse. She and her husband took apples from their orchard and
made frequent trips to the cider mill in town. These excursions gave her
great access to all newsworthy items including births, deaths, weddings,
work bees and any unsubstantiated yet interesting rumours. She was not
surprised when Annie came to her. It was no secret that May Jacques was

quite nosy. But Mrs. Allenby felt justified in keeping people informed just as long as she spoke the truth.

"Yes, Annie, you're quite right. There was an accident at the mill shortly after Charles Press and John Hewitt bought it. Let me see...," she pondered, rubbing her chin and dropping the apple she was holding in her other hand in a nearby basket. "That would have been about eight to ten years ago. But it wasn't a fire. No, it was a drowning. Martha and Charles had an infant son...ah...James, I believe his name was. Somehow he got out of his mother's sight long enough to toddle over to the millpond and tumble in. Most folks thought the parents would never be right after that. Within a short while, John sold his share of the mill to Charles—never really did find out why, though."

"Do many people know about this?" Annie asked.

"No, not really, certainly not the details, they were kept hush-hush. Only those who go to the cemetery on a regular basis might notice the small grave. Mostly the older folks might remember, I would imagine, but they're kind enough not to talk about it for Martha and Charles' sake. They're a lovely couple. It was a shame, a darn shame," Mrs. Allenby said with genuine feeling. "That's probably why they didn't have any more. Just couldn't face starting over," she added.

"Well, I must be on my way," Annie replied, feeling she had all the information she needed. That evening she related the story to her mother. In a way, May was surprised not to have known about this, but in another way she was not. When she herself had suddenly fallen ill, she missed a few years of "living" while she battled her own health problems. She was reminded of the fact that she had been confined to a wheelchair for over eleven years. It started to make sense now, the way Martha and Charles had taken Thomas into their home and treated him like their own. Mrs. Jacques decided not to mention this incident to her son.

By the third week in August, Mary had learned that Miss McGuire would not be returning to teach that fall. She had overheard Mrs. Jacques say to her husband, "Imagine that teacher questioning the school trustees. A rule is a rule. Women teachers who marry will be dismissed. In my opinion a married woman's place is in the home looking after her husband." Then Mary heard the clicking of the knitting needles. That meant she was finished speaking and no-one else would dare make a comment.

Mary was upset by the news but grateful to be forewarned before the first day back to school. The new teacher, Mr. Fitchett, was nice enough but did not compare to Miss McGuire. For one thing, he did not appreciate her poetry writing nearly as much. And he did not approve of Christmas pageants, scavenger hunts and games in general. He felt they wasted time better spent on "the books." Mary found her love for school diminishing.

At the same time, things were changing in the Jacques household. Thomas, who lately preferred to be called Tom, had moved out and Chris was rarely home because of his long work hours. Unfortunately for Mary, Annie was still there a great deal. And she relentlessly picked away at Mary. With each passing day, Mary would mull over the same question. "What am I going to do? Should I run away to the bog in the fifty acre swamp?" But what would she do? She shared her despair with only one other—Mustard.

By early October, however, a totally unexpected change came over Annie. She was unusually cheerful and actually nice to Mary at times. She even brought sweets home from town for her without any apparent reason. The personality change in Annie was nothing short of incredible.

As well, Annie developed a renewed interest in Sunday worship. She would get upset if for some reason the family did not attend and she began to spend more time "preparing" herself before leaving the house. Mary's suspicions were confirmed as the story began to unfold.

It seems that Elias Zinkan, a thirty-seven-year-old confirmed bachelor who attended St. Paul's regularly, had begun to sit with the Jacques family on Sunday morning. God moves in mysterious ways and so the courtship began.

Mary met Mr. Zinkan when he was invited to the house for Sunday dinner. While the parents approved of Annie's suitor, her brothers were not the least bit interested. As for Mary, she was curious. In due time she learned that Elias Zinkan had lived near Innerkip all his life and quietly farmed a small parcel of land. A shy, very introverted man, he had found it difficult to socialize and meet people. Mary suspected that Annie was the

Courting and "sparking" usually pre-
ceded a couple's getting married. Sunday
was the day for courtship, during a walk
home from the church or a buggy ride.
The carrying of a bouquet of flowers was
believed to bring good luck to a bride.
Barry Hoskins, Heritage Cards.

first girl he'd been "sweet on." For that matter, he was probably Annie's first and only beau. Mary was not overly impressed with his looks but very impressed with the transformation she saw in Annie. In front of her gentleman friend, Annie was especially nice to Mary.

That Christmas season brought a touch more happiness into the Jacques household. The boys cut down a spruce tree, which made its home in the parlour and the family decorated it with cran-berries and popcorn. Even Mary was included this year. Children brought their skates to school so they could enjoy the frozen river during their lunch hour. Josie lent Sarah's skates to Mary so she could enjoy the sport with her.

As usual, her much-anticipated Christmas package arrived from Scotland and Mary opened it with her usual excitement. She could never wait until December 25, and perhaps it made sense. Carolyn often sent something to keep Mary warm and she needed it once the weather turned bitter. This year she had knit her a red scarf with a fancy trim—quite a large scarf, but Carolyn had no idea how small Mary was for her age. Mary loved it just the same and knew that particularly in the winter the extra length would keep her warmer.

Carolyn's letter was filled with bubbly family news, making Mary homesick as she read. By now William was almost five; Rachel, whom they had nearly lost to scarlet fever, was three; and they had a new little one, Ruth, born this past August.

Carolyn never forgot to mention Will, John and Emma before signing off. Mary saved the letter, tucking it safely away with all the rest, in the little tea caddy she had found in the barn five years ago. From time to time when she was lonely she would read them, but often they made her feel lonelier.

Annie continued being nice to Mary. It would appear that having a beau agreed with her. One day while Mary cleaned up the kitchen she could hear Mr. Zinkan in the parlour. Having cleared his throat several times, he began to speak in a shaky, reedy voice to Annie's parents, assembled there at Annie's request. "I have asked Mr. Jacques for his daughter's hand in marriage and he has agreed." He paused for a breath and continued, "Annie and I have decided to have a Christmas wedding. We've discussed this with Reverend Ward and set a date, December 21st." Annie was beaming, a look that was becoming more common, and certainly one welcome to Mary.

Both Mr. and Mrs. Jacques seemed pleased. After all, Annie was turning twenty-three in February and most girls were "spoken for" by the age of seventeen. But no-one was happier than Mary. She firmly believed that her life would improve with Annie gone. After all, it was Annie who criticized everything she did, from baking bread to drying apples to just plain setting the table. How many times had she burned herself at the hearth trying to please Annie? Mary was always blamed if the fire went out by morning for it was she who banked the coals with ashes at night. It was Annie who always managed to find a job for Mary whenever she saw her playing outside. There was always a woodbox or water pail to fill. If Annie could not find a job to be done, with great sarcasm she would say "My lady, you get to bed, or you won't get up in the morning."

Lately, Mary had been giving a lot of thought to her brother's words about being on his own at sixteen. For Mary that was only three years away. At first, the idea of being on her own scared her but after last Christmas, she had decided that leaving was her only choice if things did not improve.

She reflected back to the previous December as she put on her thin, black shawl and went outside to fetch more kindling for the fire. It had been the night of the Cider and Sleigh Bell Ride. December the…, Mary paused, trying to remember the exact date. Thinking aloud, she said, "December the 21st." Of course, that was why the date set for Annie's wedding had stuck in her mind.

Mary shivered. The cold brought her back to reality. She hurried inside, opened the stove door and threw the wood into the fire box. Sitting by the stove, she rubbed her hands together to get warm. As the added wood ignited, she felt the instant warmth and the memories of the past came alive:

It was a frosty, very wintry night a year ago, December 21, 1896—a night best forgotten. The sleigh ride was to begin at seven o'clock at the community hall. The Jacques told Mary she could go and that she was allowed to ride in the Chesneys' bob sleigh. The Chesneys went to the sleigh ride each year as one of their Christmas traditions. Josie had been going since she was a tiny baby but this year was different. It was their first Christmas without Jimmy and the strain was evident on all the family.

Mary was so happy that she would be joining them. It was her first sleigh ride experience and Josie shared her excitement. The girls talked of nothing but this for weeks prior to the event.

"Only nine more days! Wait till you taste the hot apple cider with cinnamon sticks. The sleigh ride will be so much fun. You're going love it. I hope there'll be lots of snow."

"What happens if there isn't?"

"Don't worry," Josie said smiling, unconsciously twisting one of her flaming red braids. "Sleighs are okay even if there's only a little bit of snow."

"But what if there's no snow?" Mary persisted.

"Well, Pa said one year that happened and they used wagons instead. Either way, Mary, we'll be there."

That satisfied her and the conversation moved on to what they would wear. While Josie's clothes were not fancy, coming from a large family she never seemed to be without, like Mary. Josie always reminded Mary that her clothes were hand-me-downs from her sisters and very little had been store bought.

"This year I get to wear the blue coat and hat that Sarah wore last year," Josie explained. "It has real white pretend fur on the brim of the hat."

Ice skating on a frozen pond was a popular winter pastime for both children and adults living in rural Ontario. Often girls wore a fur "muff" to keep their hands warm. *Barry Hoskins, Heritage Cards.*

"How can it be real and pretend?" Mary asked.

"I knew you'd ask me that. It's not real fur, but it sure looks like it. I forgot to tell you the best part. It has a matching muff. I'm going to feel real special 'cause I've never had a muff before."

Mary didn't even know what a muff was, but Josie soon educated her on that subject. She concluded by telling her it was like the red velvet one in the window of Mrs. Begg's drygoods store. Sometimes Josie forgot that Mary did not get to go into town as often as she did. Mary simply nodded as if she had seen it.

"And I also have a secret that I can't tell right now," whispered an excited Josie. She was referring to the little brown fur muff that Ruth, her other sister had outgrown and agreed to lend to Mary the night of the sleigh ride.

"When will you tell me?" asked Mary.

"The night of the sleigh ride you'll find out," she replied mysteriously.

The morning of December 21 Mary jumped out of bed and ran to the tiny window in the loft. Icicles were hanging over the top of the window and several inches of snow had fallen in the night. *"Oh, thank you, thank you,"* she said as she pressed her fingers to her lips and made a kissing sound.

The day seemed longer than most. At six o'clock she quickly tidied the kitchen in order to be ready on time.

"The floor needs sweeping and the fire needs to be tended before you get

any ideas about leaving," Mrs. Jacques said to her. The others were dressing in preparation for the night's outing and Mary had hoped she'd be given a few minutes to get ready. But rather than argue, she picked up the broom and swept the floor. In her haste, as she turned to go outside to fill the woodbox, she accidentally knocked a little blue and yellow plate off the table. It smashed into tiny fragments on the plank floor.

"Now see what you've done! You're so careless. You've broken one of my favourite dishes." Mrs. Jacques sharp tongue spit the words out. "If you think you can rush through your chores just to go to this sleigh ride, you're wrong. You'll stay right here tonight where you belong and maybe you'll think twice before breaking something that doesn't belong to you."

"But it was an accident, Ma'am. I'm sorry, really I am." Mary would have said anything at that point, just to be able to go. She dropped to her knees and began picking up the pieces. "Maybe I can fix it. Please let me go. I really am sorry."

"Sorry won't bring back my plate. You'd best stay home and think about what you did."

Mary knew from past experiences that once Mrs. Jacques had made up her mind, nothing would change it. It was pointless to argue. She got up slowly and let the pieces she had been holding in her apron fall to the floor for a second time.

Three days after Christmas she saw Josie who admitted her disappointment when the Jacques arrived at the sleigh ride without Mary. She told Mary about the little brown muff she had planned to lend to her for the evening. "But don't worry, Mary, Ma said I could bring it to school and you can wear it all day if you want."

Throughout the years Mary had never confided in Josie about her unhappiness living with the Jacques and how badly they treated her, especially Mrs. Jacques. That day it simply poured out of her uncontrollably.

"It's so terrible, Jos. I don't know what to do. Daniel's the only one who is ever nice to me," she sobbed quietly when she finished her story.

"Have you talked to Reverend Ward?" she asked, putting her arm around her. She was not exactly surprised at what Mary said, having been suspicious for a long time. "Maybe he can help."

"No, Jos, I can't tell anyone and you mustn't either. Mrs. Jacques would be so mad, things would only get worse," and she quickly wiped the tears from her eyes.

"School starts up again soon, Mary. Maybe things will get better."

"If they don't, I'm leaving when I turn sixteen just like Will did."

"But if you leave, we'd never see each other again." Josie confided.

"I'd still see you, Jos." Mary paused. "Somehow."

Mary was staring at the stove deep in thought when Annie popped her head into the room. "For heaven sakes, it's freezing in here. Look at the fire, it must be nothing but a bed of coals. Surely you can do better than that."

That memory had been played out once again in her mind, but she wished it could be extinguished as easily as the fire. Throwing on her shawl, she went outside where the air was brisk but not as icy as Annie's tone.

She took in a big breath, paused, then slowly exhaled. Two wedding announcements in such a short period of time: first Miss McGuire's and now Annie's. Mary believed that good news often follows bad news. When she'd heard Miss McGuire was leaving the school, she was hopeful something good might happen. It did; Annie was leaving home in nineteen days.

Sixteen

MARY LOSES A FRIEND

"There was, of course, no attempt by such men,
who were usually immigration agents anyway, to
inquire into the child's feelings—the things of the
heart—for in the Canada of that time a child was
not seen to have hopes and dreams and a personality that could be hurt, sometimes beyond restoring.
A child was, after all, an incomplete person, a pil-
grim on his way to becoming human; until he
reached adult years he did not really have an inner
life of the emotions or the mind."[36]

January, 1898

MARY HAD hoped that life at the Jacques would become more tolerable
after Annie left home. For several weeks Mrs. Jacques was moody and
sullen. She complained that she now lived in a household of men and had
much more responsibility. According to her "everything was going to pot."
She constantly talked about being lonely and missing her only daughter.
It was as if she had forgotten that before her marriage, Annie was working
full time and rarely home during the day. Mary did all the chores then and
was still doing them. In fact, nothing had changed in the daily routine, yet
Mrs. Jacques persistently perceived things to be different.

As the days passed, she became more demanding of Mary's attention. She was so unhappy that finally the doctor was summoned. He could find no specific physical ailment beyond her usual moribund condition but suggested that perhaps Mrs. Jacques needed more rest.

Mrs. Jacques now insisted on having Mary comb and brush her hair every night, often for as long as two hours. Sometimes Mary felt as though her arms were going to break. Soon she began to pretend she was sick after school. It meant no supper, but it also meant she did not have to pamper Mrs. Jacques and entertain her for the evening. Mary tried not to be too sick or sick too frequently or she would not be allowed to go to school the next day. School remained Mary's escape. The friendships developed there were the most important thing in her life, that and Mustard.

Although winter was not her favourite season, the snow did provide lots of fun at school. South of the schoolhouse was the land owned by Mr. Allenby. It dipped down to what people referred to as the "flats." Using a smooth block of wood from the woodpile, the children would toboggan down this slope with great glee. Last spring, Mary had watched a group of energetic boys dig a tunnel into the side of this hill, part of their creation of a "secret" cave. All went well until one day later that year, when Mr. Allenby's cattle were grazing on the hill, the tunnel collapsed, taking a cow with it. The farmer was furious. This knoll was later bought by the school board, the slope levelled and the soil used to fill up a low spot on the school grounds.[37]

Each year by spring breakup, the flats would be flooded with water and, since the school grounds were low near the road, the schoolhouse would stand on an island. Mary always loved the challenge of climbing along the fence to get to school. If you got your feet wet, you could dry them by the large wood stove. Sometimes you even got a holiday, if the water was high enough.

When things were particularly bad at home, Mary found great comfort in thinking about the little stone schoolhouse and the memories it housed. As time went by she found herself confiding in Josie more and more. But it was a vicious circle. She would sense Josie getting upset and since her friend was unable to help her in any way, Mary would feel guilty for having mentioned her troubles. But still, Josie was her only outlet.

One day in mid-February, Mary told Josie that she did not see how she could stand it anymore. "Don't be surprised if one day I don't show up for school. I might be gone."

"Mary, you wouldn't leave without saying good-bye, would you?" Josie asked as her big green eyes filled.

Mary was immediately sorry for what she had said. "No, of course, I wouldn't, Jos. It's just that it's so hard. I thought it would be better with Annie gone. In some ways it's worse. Mrs. Jacques used to sit and talk to Annie in the evening. Now I have to comb her hair or read to her until she falls asleep. Even on Sunday when no-one's supposed to read, I still have to read to her. I'm so tired of rules that are only meant for me, nobody else."

"What kind of rules, Mary?"

"Oh, if I'm called I better come right away. I wouldn't dare be called a second time. But if the boys are called and they don't answer, nothing happens. Everybody else gets served first at the table. I have to wait for it to be passed, I'm never to ask. But if others ask, that's all right. It's always that way, every day."

"I had no idea it was like that all the time. Please let me talk to Ma and Pa. Maybe they can help."

"Jos, you promised you wouldn't say anything," Mary pleaded, already regretting her confessions.

"I know. But I didn't know it was this bad. What have you got to lose?"

"Plenty! If she finds out she won't let me finish my last year of school and I won't ever see you again. You don't want that, do you?" Mary said exactly what she knew would stop Josie from telling anyone her secrets. Already she had decided that in two years when she turned sixteen she was gone. And legally no-one could stop her, not even Mrs. Jacques. The real question was, could she survive the ordeal that long?

Mary realized that she would have to be more careful about what she told her friend in future. She just had to learn to cope with things herself. Thank heavens for Mustard, she thought as she tramped through the snow that icy cold winter afternoon on her way home from school. She could tell the cat absolutely anything and be certain it was kept a secret.

Upon her arrival at the farm, she went straight to the barn to find her friend. What a shock not to find the cat curled up in his usual spot at the far end of the loft between the two mows of hay!

"Mustard, where are you? We really need to talk," Mary scolded as though she were a schoolteacher. She hunted everywhere in the loft, climbed down the ladder and looked behind the buggy wheels, another one of Mustard's favourite haunts. No sign of her friend. After about twenty minutes of searching, it was no longer a game.

Mary went in the house, changed her clothes and started her evening chores of fetching wood and water, setting the table and scrubbing vegetables. She could not get him out of her mind. Lately Mustard had been sleeping much of the time and Mary wondered if her friend was sick. She would take special treats out to the barn and often they would be left untouched. It never occurred to Mary that Mustard was getting old. She searched before and after school, day after day without success.

When five days passed and Mustard was still missing, Mary was really worried. She took a shortcut home from school, cutting through Mr. Riddell's stump fence, across his field and into the woods behind his farm. Mrs. Jacques had forbidden her to do this, but she was feeling particularly anxious to find her pet. She wanted to get home sooner to have more time to look for Mustard before dark.

As she hurried through the tall trees, she thought she spotted something just beyond some bushy shrubs. She approached cautiously and then she saw the missing cat. Mustard was curled up in a small ball, completely protected in the low fork of a large tree trunk, partially covered by snow-laden branches. Mustard looked as though he were sleeping, but Mary knew this was not so.

She moved closer and, as her feet crunched through the icy snow, her heart

Stumps from the pioneer days of clearing land, were often used to make fences. *From* Fences.[38]

pounded. Her mind raced back to something Miss McGuire had said about how animals prepare for death. She knelt down and gently touched the cat. Its body was cold. And she knew that Mustard was gone. She stood and stared for the longest time. Then she took off her red wool scarf, the Christmas gift Carolyn had sent her that year, and wrapped it tightly around one of the tree branches.

She ran the rest of the way home, sobbing violently, tears stinging her already chilled face. By the time she got there, there were no more tears. Mary found a small wooden box in the barn and quickly returned to the spot she had marked.

She buried Mustard that cold winter day in February, lining the box with her scarf before carefully laying her friend inside. She put the box in the resting place where Mustard had chosen to die and covered it with tree branches and a fresh layer of snow so nothing would be visible to a stranger tramping through the woods. The last thing she did was place two sticks from a fallen branch on top of the snow in the shape of a cross. She said her good-byes and promised to visit regularly.

She walked home slowly, feeling emotionally drained. Mrs. Jacques was waiting for her at the door. "You're late, Girl! What have you been doing? I could be half frozen for all you care. We need wood for the fire so don't bother taking your coat off."

Mary turned to go out again, saying nothing.

"And where is your scarf? I suppose you've gone and lost that too!"

Mary turned back, looked at Mrs. Jacques right in the eye and very bravely said, "No, Ma'am, I gave it to my best friend."

Seventeen

FREEDOM AT LAST

"There were many things in that generation which,
by today's standards, seem quite dreadful. But you
cannot simply say that and leave it there. You must
judge all of these things against the backdrop of the
time in which they took place—the attitudes toward
child care, the limitations of staff, the limitations of
facilities, the limitations of funding. And along with
that there was the almost overwhelming pressure to
take more and more children into care, so you had
to move more and more out of the Homes and place
them elsewhere, often, in the case of Bernardo's and
other such groups, in Canada. But their great concern, which we should not forget, was to give the
child a better chance—a better chance than he
would have if he stayed in the circumstances in
which he was at the time."[39]

July 25, 1900

IS IT irony or pure coincidence that a little girl born in Rutherglen, Scotland should cross the ocean as an orphan and end up in the small community of Innerkip, named after a river flowing through Renfrewshire,

Scotland? An Innerkip resident, Mrs. Barwick, had come from Inverkip, Renfrewshire, Scotland by the river "Kip" and named the post office Innerkip. It really should have been "Inverkip" but was recorded "Innerkip," and the name stuck.[40]

And in similar fashion to her leaving Rutherglen eleven years before, she packed her small, red valise and left Innerkip. But that is where the similarity ends.

She was taken from her home in Scotland and sent to London. It was a decision made suddenly by others. Today, Mary was leaving Innerkip, uncertain of her destination but she had made the decision by herself— the culmination of eight years of personal heartache and suffering. This time Mary was not leaving family behind.

She had found it difficult to say her final good-bye to Mustard when she went to the woods the previous day. It had been two and a half years since her cat had died, but there was something comforting about being physically near where she had laid him to rest, something safe about the woods that she was going to miss.

What she would not miss was Mrs. Jacques's sharp criticism and the twelve to fifteen hour days she spent doing heavy and often tedious jobs assigned to her ever since she finished school two years ago. Sometimes the work left her physically exhausted and sometimes ill by nightfall. And then there were the accidents that Mrs. Jacques referred to as mishaps. Mary had the scars to prove it.

Worse than any of this was the desperate loneliness and depression that she had suffered for eight long years. But the last two years had brought about the most significant changes for Mary.

She had faced puberty alone, a somewhat frightening journey from childhood to young adulthood even for those who have support. Without Josie's help Mary would have been lost, even though Josie was a year younger.

Daniel got a job at the sawmill in town and was hardly ever home any-more. She had always cared about him the most and felt she had lost a friend. Since finishing school, Mary's life had seemed empty and futile.

Staying home all day with Mrs. Jacques was more than Mary could bear, especially with the many changes since Annie moved out. May Jacques' bitterness grew, her health continued to deteriorate and almost daily there would be some new malaise. Day by day she became more and more dependent on Mary.

Josie, being a year younger than Mary, had gone back to school after Mary left, but admitted it was just was not the same without her. Given an opportunity to apprentice with Miss Kelland, the local seamstress, she left in the middle of the school year. Over the years Josie had won several ribbons in the fairs for her beautiful stitchery and handwork, and Mary was happy for her. But already, without school as their meeting place, their times together became fewer and fewer.

As she hurried down the lonely county road, the words of her brother kept coming back to her. For a brief moment she closed her eyes and could see the determination in Will's face as he slapped the ball into his gloved hand, "Once I turn sixteen I'll be on my own."

Mary just could not chance it and wait for her sixteenth birthday just a week away. If ever there was a perfect day for her to take her leaving, it was today. Mr. Jacques was raking hay in the back field, the boys were at work and Mrs. Jacques was preoccupied with some rare company.

Quietly packing her meagre belongings, she surreptitiously slipped down the stairs and out the kitchen door, making sure she could not be seen from the parlour window. Luck was on her side. Just a short distance along the gravel road, Mary managed to hitch a ride into town with the Lindsays, an elderly couple who had offered her rides in the past which she had always declined. Today she accepted.

"Thank you very much, Sir. I'm grateful for the lift," Mary said politely as she stepped up into the buggy.

"And where might you be heading, dear?" asked Mrs. Lindsay, more for conversation than curiosity, Mary hoped.

"Well, Ma'am, I'm catching the train to...Stratford," Mary said as she patted the suitcase lying on her lap. While not sure of where she was headed, it was important not to arouse suspicion.

"You have lots of time, since the train doesn't leave until 11:10, dear" the woman replied kindly. Mary smiled. She already knew that because she had gone to the station once with Mr. Jacques to pick up Annie and had put to memory the Sunday train schedule.

Once they pulled up in front of Watkins' general store, Mary thanked them for the ride and off she went in the direction of the train station.

The main street of a village was the hub of activity. Shops included a general
store, post office, tailor, harness and wagon shops, the cooperage and at least one
hotel. The doctor, the undertaker (usually the furniture maker) and the school
and churches would be found near the centre of town. *Courtesy Dufferin County
Museum and Archives.*

"My, what a wisp of a thing she is, Henry!" exclaimed his wife. "I wonder why she'd be travelling so far alone—maybe meeting a distant relative, poor child."

"Never you mind, Isabel. It's none of our affair," he replied brusquely
and maneouvered his wife toward the store.

Mary walked determinedly as though she had a mission to accomplish
and indeed she did. She went to the post office in Mrs. Begg's store. To
date, Sara Beggs had the longest term in office, having been postmistress
for thirty years, since 1870. Later, when she did retire in 1907, local villagers would comment it was more than coincidence that she relinquished
her job the year before rural mail delivery service was inaugurated.

Mrs. Beggs managed to run a smooth operation in the postal service as
well as in dry goods. She was an efficient, hard-working lady who kept
abreast of all the happenings in town. Why, she even knew that Thomas
Perry, the courier who had brought mail to Strathallan and Innerkip, used
to knit socks as he drove along. One year he knit seven pair en route for
Christmas gifts.[41]

In 1881, railway mail service was introduced and couriers became a
thing of the past. "Somehow it lost its personal touch," Mrs. Beggs sadly
lamented. Railways were paid for transporting mail on a space basis, at

A view along the main street of Innerkip, showing Trachsel's hotel, the first store and the harness shop. The first hotel to open in the village in 1856 was known as the Edward Hart Inn. *From* The Early Days of Innerkip District.

so much per running mile. The first contractors for conveying mail between the station at Innerkip and the post office walked and carried the mail bag on their backs. When William Waugh became the contractor, he used a carryall and conveyed passengers as well as mail. This horse-drawn covered carryall was a convenience as well to the travelling public since the station was half a mile from the centre of town.[42]

The carryall was just leaving the post office as Mary entered the store, but it did not matter. She would not have taken a ride anyway, since it meant more questions would have to be answered.

Mrs. Beggs never missed a thing and Mary certainly did not want to be part of her latest story. If mailing this letter were not so important, she would not have gone to the post office at all. Approaching the counter, she produced a small, white piece of paper, folded in thirds and sealed with wax. Mrs. Beggs prided herself on knowing who everyone was in town and was taken aback that the girl did not look familiar. For once, Mary was thankful that she had rarely been in town and, although the postmistress would have heard about the girl living at the Jacques, it was unlikely that she would recognize Mary.

"And what have we here, Miss...?" she paused, waiting for Mary to reveal her name.

"Please, Ma'am, it's a letter for Josie Chesney," Mary replied timidly.

"Would that be Dr. Chesney's family?" she asked, knowing full well that it was not. If she detained the girl briefly, maybe she could discover her identity.

"No, Ma'am, Dr. Chesney is Josie's uncle. Her father's name is Oliver and they live on the sixteenth line."

"Oh, of course, dear. And if I may be so bold, who might you be?" Mrs. Begg's curiosity was getting the better of her.

"Just a friend, a friend of the family passing through. I'd sure appreciate it if you could see that she gets this letter, Ma'am."

"Of course," Mrs. Beggs said coldly and reached out to take it.

Mary handed her the letter and a half cent. She knew all about postage stamps; they had studied it in school. She watched while the woman put a half-penny black stamp on her letter, then hurried out. At that moment Mrs. Beggs was probably holding it up to the window to get a better look at it, a letter written from the heart and only intended for Josie. It told of her desperation and loneliness and it apologized for leaving without a proper good-bye. The letter was unsigned just in case it fell into the wrong hands. If it reached Josie, there would be no doubt in her mind as to the sender. She just hoped Josie would understand.

The only other person Mary was concerned about was Will. She knew when she left Innerkip it meant it was impossible for him to come for her; however, she could wait for him no longer, nor could she live with the Jacques one more day.

Once she got settled somewhere and got a job, she would contact Mr. Murray in Stratford to see if he knew Will's whereabouts, or John's. But Mary had little faith in him. She had given up on finding Emma since she was sent so far away. She dreamed about travelling back to Scotland to see Carolyn too, but knew that was probably never going to happen.

Mary headed for the station with the same determination that had helped her get this far. She never looked back. When she arrived at the wicket, she found she had enough money, the money Will had given her, to go as far as London. And that is how she decided on her destination. The station master could not help wondering where the little curly-haired young woman with the straw hat and tiny red suitcase was really heading as he helped her board the train.

With the exception of one elderly man and a couple, there was no-one else aboard. Mary chose a window seat and felt wistful but not sad as the train pulled out. She watched the fields roll by and allowed herself to be gently lulled by the slow lateral motion of the train rolling down the tracks.

After about thirty minutes the train stopped at Beachville to pick up some passengers and mail. A young girl in her mid-twenties boarded the train and stopped beside Mary's seat. Mary panicked briefly. Was this someone from Innerkip who recognized her?

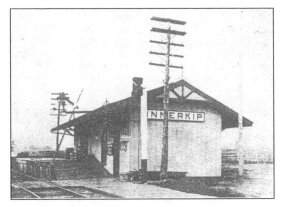

The first railway station at Innerkip. About 1875 the building of the Credit Valley Railway from Toronto to St. Thomas was begun at both ends of the line. The two sets of labourers met between Innerkip and Woodstock and the track was opened in 1879. Excursions were organized to give as many as possible an opportunity to try the luxuries of this new mode of travel. *From* The Early Days of Innerkip District *by Zella Hotson.*

"Do you mind if I sit with you?" she asked.

"No, I don't mind," Mary replied.

"I've a long trip ahead and I hate travelling alone," the girl admitted, smiling as she sat down, removing her large brimmed hat and setting a train case in the aisle beside her. Mary guessed the girl was around Annie's age but nothing like Annie. This young woman was friendly.

"Where are you going?" Mary asked with curiousity.

"I go as far as London, then I catch another train to Montreal," the girl explained, still a bit out of breath from hurrying. "I'm to meet my cousin Elizabeth there. She's coming to live with us," she said excitedly. "What about you?"

"I'm going to London," Mary answered truthfully. "My sister Carolyn just had a baby and she needs me," she said without hesitation. She turned and looked out the window.

And I will be free, she thought.

Cornfields, pastures, rivers and trees flashed past but all Mary could see was her own reflection in the glass.

BACKGROUND
TO
MARY JANEWAY

THEY WERE called the "home children," those thousands of children, some of them orphans, some fatherless, some destitute, who were sent from England to Canada between 1869 and 1948, in hopes that they might find a better life. Some did. Many did not. This story is based on a real person, a person who entered my life when I was very young. I have never forgotten her and hope that my telling of *Mary Janeway: The Legacy of a Home Child* will further illuminate our collective understanding of child immigration, a little documented period in Canadian history.

The early days of Home Children in the 1870s, 80s and 90s occurred at a time when many settlers were still struggling to establish stable households. Cash was a scarce commodity. For many, times in rural Ontario were less than prosperous.

I believe my story reflects these hardships and deprivation of early settlement at the turn of the century in rural Ontario. Rather than assign blame for actions to characters in this book, the story delineates their often desperate determination to survive, frequently under trying circumstances.

I am not sure what it was exactly that finally possessed me to tell her story. Perhaps it was the gold ring that I wear on my fourth finger and twist nervously when I'm deep in thought. The ring belonged to Mary's daughter.

The inscription inside reads "Mother to Mona Xmas, 1913." Or could it have been the bookmark that I found in Mary's Bible, that her son Ross had made when he was in kindergarten? In any case, the telling of this story was long overdue.

I can't honestly describe the first encounter I had with Mary Janeway because I was six days old when we met. She came home from the hospital with me as a visiting homemaker from the Red Feather Organization. Slowly, she became an integral part of our family and assumed the role of a grandmother. We needed her as much as she needed us. My family, including my parents called her Mrs. Church. No-one ever referred to her as Mary.

I remember when my brother John was born. I was five and my sister Catharine was almost eight.

Mary Church (Janeway) was godmother to the author. This photograph was taken on the steps of the church just after the christening ceremony. From left to right: Mary Church (Janeway), Gladys Hewson, Robert Hewson, Catharine (age 3) and Mary Hewson (now Pettit). *Courtesy the Hewson Collection.*

Mrs. Church moved into our home for awhile and simply kept a busy household running smoothly. She was always with us on special occasions like baptisms, graduations and birthdays and, consequently, was in a great number of family photographs. She was a small woman—that is, short and, by then, a little on the plump side. She had steely grey wisps of fine hair and wore a little pillbox hat, with soft netting that fell across her forehead. As far as I can remember, she always wore a hat, even if we were just going on a picnic.

If we were only going to the store, the park or even for a short walk, Mrs. Church hated to be left behind. Perhaps that was because she lived alone and had no family of her own. At least, that is what I thought at the time.

Once my brother, sister and I grew a little older, I thought we would see less of her. But just the opposite happened! My dad would usually pick her up on Friday night after he left school and she would spend the weekend with us. Sometimes I would go with him to get her. I can't remember a Friday evening when she wasn't sitting outside on the steps of her rooming house, wearing her coat and hat and clutching her purse, ready and waiting with her small blue suitcase sitting beside her. The look on her face when she saw us arrive made the anticipation of her visit all the more exciting. This is my most vivid childhood memory of Mary Janeway.

As time passed, I grew more attached to her. A pattern was established whereby she would come almost every weekend, always on special calendar days, and often her visits would slide into the weekdays. It was simple; we didn't want her to leave and she didn't want to go home. Home is probably the wrong word to use since it usually refers to a place where one likes to be. About every two years, Mrs. Church changed her residence; either the rent was increased or the conditions became intolerable. Please do not misunderstand me. Mrs. Church wasn't a complainer; she would merely say, "It was a little far from the bus stop, you know."

A typical weekend included shopping Saturday morning, a bowl of homemade oxtail soup for lunch, an afternoon walk, a big dinner, popcorn and TV. The way that Mrs. Church kept up with the pace of my family, it was hard to believe that she was over seventy. I have a feeling that we packed more activities than usual into our days when she was with us. My mother would often suggest that she rest or stay home to avoid some of our more strenuous outings. Her reply was always the same: "No, I wouldn't mind going. The exercise is good for me," or, "I'm sure the fresh air will do me a world of good."

Mrs. Church always stated her case and, in a nice way, made it clear what she intended to do. I can still see her sitting on a little stool at the long, low family room windows, peeling potatoes or apples, podding peas or pitting cherries in preparation for Sunday's dinner. Why, I'm sure if it hadn't been for Mrs. Church, we would not have had half the fruit pies that we did. She was always so willing to help. Imagine two women in one kitchen and never a harsh word!

Sunday evenings were a bit quiet. I always felt as though a big dark cloud was hovering over us. When my dad would drive her back into the city, I usually did not go with them because I found it so difficult to part. It seemed easier to say goodbye at our house than to drive down those narrow, dark city streets and watch her climb the stairs to a poor, run-down rooming house.

Now that I am older, I often wonder if she would have liked to come and live with us. It was never discussed, and I feel that if the subject had come up she would have politely refused. Mrs. Church was a woman of great pride. She had paid her dues, worked her entire life and was not about to become dependent in her later years. I would hear her say to my parents, "I know my own place; that is very important. I never want to intrude on someone. I only want to be where I am wanted."

It was when I heard conversations like this that I began to wonder about her past. For the longest time I was

Mary Church (Janeway), June 1954. The author's memories of Mary Janeway are of Mrs. Church as an adult in her more mature years. *Courtesy the Hewson Collection.*

too young to give it much thought but as I grew, so did my questions. I realized that she had lived a sad and difficult life.

I recall one particular evening having difficulty falling asleep. I was twelve. I started downstairs, but stopped halfway because of a conversation I overheard between my parents. They were talking about Mrs. Church, so I sat on the stairs in the dark and listened. They were discussing her childhood, how hard she'd been worked, how little she'd been loved and how strong she must have been to survive. My father said, "Mrs. Church has had an interesting life...somebody should write a book about her." I decided right there in the middle of the night that once I was grown up, I would do just that.

Joseph Jacques, grandson of Daniel Jacques, standing outside his Innerkip home in August, 1999. *Photo by Paul Pettit.*

It was then that I started to ask my father questions about Mrs. Church's past. I was an inquisitive child and my father knew that I was not easily pacified. He told me he'd begun to write things down and even taped a conversation with her on a reel-to-reel tape recorder. I was thankful to have these tangibles at a later date when I began to put my own thoughts on paper. At the same time, I began to put to memory my conversations with Mrs. Church, often thinking about her stories when I was alone.

I remember the weekend I stayed with her; I couldn't have been more than thirteen or fourteen. I packed a small bag and my dad took me into the city for a visit, immersing me in her world. There, I got to stay up late and drink Ovaltine in a cup and saucer, and listen to her voice as I looked at all her treasures and nic-nacs.

I became aware that she'd experienced almost a whole lifetime of living before I had even met her. She had a story attached to every trinket in her room and the kind of memories which one only accumulates with great passages of time.

My curiousity really began here in this one-room dwelling of hers, with a bathroom down the hall. While she was reluctant to talk about certain aspects of her past, I soon realized that the things she valued the most were the things that were absent in her own childhood. Mary would never have believed that her life was worth writing about, for in her mind it wasn't even worth discussing.

After her death in 1964, I asked my father for his notes and the recording of her voice. I tucked them away in a safe place.

Years later, I went to Innerkip where Mary had lived with the Jacques family. At the post office I discovered there was one living relative of the family that I'd grown curious to learn more about. His name was Joseph L. Jacques. I called him from a phone booth, introduced myself and asked if I could visit him. In May, 1991, I met Joseph Jacques, the eighty-year-old grandson of Daniel Jacques.

He was a delightful, articulate gentleman with an amazing memory. He had lived his entire life in Innerkip, not far from his grandparent's home. I learned a great deal from Mr. Jacques about his ancestors, particularly his grandmother, May Jacques. He remembered seeing Mary at his grandfather's funeral when he was eleven and she was an adult. He gave me directions to find the land where the Jacques homestead had been. On my way through town, I stopped and wandered through the Innerkip Cemetery. It helped to familiarize myself with the local family names. On the outskirts of town, I found what had been the Jacques property. All I could see was a large grove of poplar trees that Mr. Jacques said had "taken over the land" where the little clapboard house once stood. I felt a closeness to Mary and I knew that it was time to tell her story. I began to write.

I'm often asked how long it took. It took me thirty years to think about it and ten years to write it. This chronicle depicts eight years of Mary's life. Through a series of circumstances I had the privilege of knowing and loving Mary Janeway. In her later years she became my godmother and finally belonged to a family.

Mary Pettit

ENDNOTES

1   Kenneth Bagnell, *The Little Immigrants: The Orphans Who Came to Canada*. (Toronto: MacMillan of Canada, 1980) 242. All quotes opening the individual chapters are used with the permission of Kenneth Bagnell.

2   Interview with Joseph Jacques, grandson of Daniel Jacques, August 1999.

3   Kenneth Bagnell, *The Little Immigrants*, dust jacket.

4   This document was created by the author, based on research from Kenneth Bagnell's *The Little Immigrants*, and designed to highlighting attitudes prevalent in the 1800s pertaining to the discipline of young children.

5   Kenneth Bagnell, *The Little Immigrants*, 83.

6   Information for the Jacques family tree was provided by Joseph Jacques, grandson of Daniel Jacques.

7   Kenneth Bagnell, *The Little Immigrants*, 184.

8   Kenneth Bagnell, *The Little Immigrants*, 44.

9   Kenneth Bagnell, *The Little Immigrants,* dust jacket.

10   Kenneth Bagnell, *The Little Immigrants*, 213.

11   Gary Thomson, *Village Life in Upper Canada*. (Belleville, Ont.: Mika Publishing Company, 1988) 143.

12   E.C. Guillet, *The Pioneer Farmer and Backwoodsman Vol. 1*. (Toronto: The Ontario Pub-lishing Company Limited, 1963) 182.

13   Gary Thomson, *Village Life in Upper* Canada, 122.

14   Kenneth Bagnell, *The Little Immigrants*, 205.

15   The riverbank scene is taken from a book owned by the author's maternal grand-mother, Fidelia Lindsay. The book, *Thro' Wood and Field* came into her possession sometime between 1880 and 1890.

16   Both Arbour Day and Lockout Day are described by Jessie Beattie in her book, *A Walk Through Yesterday: Memoirs of Jessie L. Beattie*. (Toronto: McClelland & Stewart Limited, 1976) 64, 65.

17   Kenneth Bagnell, *The Little Immigrants*, 83.

18   According to the *World Book Encyclopedia,* the British Post Office issued its first postage stamp in 1840.

19   Gavin Hamilton Green, *The Old Log School*. (Toronto: Natural Heritage Books 1992) 178,179.

20   Kenneth Bagnell, *The Little Immigrants*, 83.

21   Adapted from documents used by inspectors who visited home children: National Archives of Canada. Microfilm reel #C-4690 Vol. 32 File 724 Part I.

22   Kenneth Bagnell, *The Little Immigrants*, dust jacket.

23   Kenneth Bagnell, *The Little Immigrants*, 33.

24   According to Zella Hotson, in her book on Innerkip, a Dr. John Taylor (1803-1884), a "Negro," lived in Innerkip and practised healing. He is said to have written a book on herbs and house remedies, a book seemingly popular with many of the local people. *The Early Days of Innerkip District*, 39.

25   Illustration of squirrels by C.W. Jeffries, from *Fences*, 68.

26   An excerpt from an early *Ontario Readers Primer*.

27   Kenneth Bagnell, *The Little Immigrants*, 240.

28   Zella Hotson, *The Early Days of Innerkip District*, 64.

29   "As soon as a person died, a number of things were traditionally done almost simultaneously: a bell was tolled announcing the death;...Most of our contacts told us that the number of times the bell tolled depended on the age of the person who died..." From *Foxfire 2*. (New York: Anchor Press / Doubleday 1973) 306, 309.

30   Kenneth Bagnell, *The Little Immigrants*, 215.

31   The tradition of the "red devil" is mentioned but not explained in Zella Hotson, *The Early Days of Innerkip District*, 73.

32   The picnic area description is from Zella Hotson, 73.

33   Kenneth Bagnell, *The Little Immigrants*, 180.

34   Taken from E.C. Guillet, *The Pioneer Farmer and Backwoodsman*, 146.

35   Kenneth Bagnell, *The Little Immigrants*, 83.

36   Ibid.

37   Zella Hotson, *The Early Days of Innerkip District*, 46.

38   From *Fences*, 15.

39   Kenneth Bagnell, *The Little Immigrants*, 239.

40   The name Innerkip means the mouth (Inver) of the Kip, a little stream which flows through Renfrewshire, Scotland. Taken from Zella Hotson, *The Early Days of Innerkip District*, 55.

41   Information on Innerkip from Zella Hotson, 56.

42   Ibid, 58.

43   Most definitions adapted from *The Canadian Oxford Dictionary*, (Katherine Barber ed.). Toronto: Oxford University Press, 1998.

GLOSSARY[43]

agate	a coloured stone; toy marble resembling streaked quartz
ague	a malarial fever, with cold, hot and sweating stages
apple snow	a dessert
bobsleigh	resembling a large wagon, only with two sets of runners rather than wheels; pulled by a team of horses
bunting	decorations such as flags, banners and streamers
catarrh	inflammation of the mucous membrane of the nose
courting	paying amorous attention to someone, dating; see also sparking
diphtheria	an acute infectious bacterial disease causing inflammation of the throat and difficulty in breathing
domestic	a household servant
galloping consumption	advanced stages of tuberculosis (t.b.)
hoops	wooden hoops rolled with a stick
infantile paralysis	poliomyelitis, commonly called polio
influenza	highly contagious virus disease, commonly called flu
Johnnycake	a cornmeal bread usually baked or fried on a griddle
linsey-woolsey	a fabric of coarse wool
muff	a tubular piece of fur with an opening at each end to allow hands to be inserted for warmth
pantaloons	men's close-fitting breeches, usually fastened below the calf or just above the knee

parlour   a sitting room, usually reserved for special guests

piggins   small wooden buckets with an extended arm for handle

pinafore   an apron-like garment, usually with buttons or ties at the back, worn over a dress, especially by small girls

quinsy   a sore throat, sometimes accompanied by fever, especially an abscess in the area around the tonsils

rickets   a disease of children caused by a deficiency of vitamin D, characterized by the softening of the bones and bow legs

scarlet fever an infectious bacterial fever characterized by high fever, sore throat and red skin rash, sometimes confused with measles, believed to weaken the heart

shinny   a forerunner to road hockey

slate   a piece of fine-grained metamorphic sedimentary rock usually framed in wood, used for writing on

smoker   a small wooden table with an ashtray in the middle, glass jars on either side to store tobacco and a place to rest a pipe.

sparking courting, dating

tea caddy usually a wooden box lined with metal used as a container for tea

typhus   an infectious fever marked by a high fever, purple rash and delirium, often transmitted by lice or fleas

BIBLIOGRAPHY

Bagnell, Kenneth, *The Little Immigrants: The Orphans Who Came to Canada*. Toronto: Macmillan of Canada, 1980.

Barber, Philip, *The Road Home: Sketches of Rural Canada*. Scarborough: Prentice-Hall of Canada Limited, 1976.

Beattie, Jessie L., *A Walk Through Yesterday: Memoirs of Jessie L. Beattie*. Toronto: McClelland & Stewart Limited, 1976.

Canadian Almanac and Miscellaneous Directory for the year 1900. Toronto: Copp Clark Company Limited, 1900.

Green, Gavin Hamilton, *The Old Log School*. Toronto: Natural Heritage Books, 1992.

Greenwood, Barbara, *A Pioneer Story*. Toronto: Kids Can Press Limited, 1994.

Guillet, E.C., *The Pioneer Farmer and Backwoodsman*. (Vol. 1 and Vol. 2) Toronto: The Ontario Publishing Company Limited (Distributed by the University of Toronto Press), 1963.

Hotson, Zella, M., *The Early Days of Innerkip District*. Privately published, 1952. (Later re-issued by the Innerkip Historical Committee, 1984.)

Kalman, Bobbie, *Historic Communities*. Niagara-on-the-Lake: Crabtree Publishing Company, 1993.

Kalman, Bobbie, *The Early Settler Life Series*. Toronto: Crabtree Publishing Company, 1991.

Seymour, John, *Rural Life*. Great Britain: Collins and Brown Limited, 1991.

Statistical Year-Book of Canada for 1901. Ottawa: 17th year of issue, issued by the Department of Agriculture, Government Printing Bureau, 1902.

Statutes of the Province of Ontario, passed in the session held in the sixtieth year of the reign of Her Magesty Queen Victoria. L.K. Cameron, printer to the Queen's most excellent Magesty, 1897.

Symons, Harry. *Fences*. Toronto: McGraw-Hill Ryerson Limited, 1958, 1974.

Thomson, Gary, *Village Life in Upper Canada*, Belleville: Mika Publishing Company, 1988.

Unitrade Specialized Catalogue of Canadian Stamps 1997 Edition. Toronto: The Unitrade Press, 1996.

ABOUT THE AUTHOR

Mary Pettit was born and raised in the Hamilton area, along with a sister and a brother. Their parents were educators. Both education and music were encouraged when she was growing up. In her family it was often said that "no-one leaves home until you can play three instruments." Mary chose the piano, violin and French horn.

She graduated from Hillfield-Strathallan College and attended Ryerson where she earned a Bachelor of Applied Arts in Radio and Television. Mary continued her studies at York University, graduating with a Bachelor of Arts in Psychology and a Bachelor of Education at Brock University.

She worked at CFTO-TV as a program co-ordinator and researcher and has done freelance work for the CTV network. She was also the judge for 'Reach for the Top' on CHCH-TV. Mary has been a teacher for the Hamilton Wentworth Board of Education for eighteen years.

Her personal interests include aerobics, tennis, skiing, playing bridge, knitting and reading. She has two daughters and lives in Stoney Creek with her husband Paul.